# CARLTON:
# DOWN SIZED

*Tawnee Chasny*

Carlton: Down Sized © 2021 Tawnee Chasny

ISBN:

| | |
|---|---|
| Paperback | 978-1-63945-025-1 |
| E-book | 978-1-63945-056-5 |

The views expressed in this book are solely those of the author and do not necessarily reflect the views of the publisher, and the publisher hereby disclaims any responsibility for them.

Writers' Branding
1800-608-6550
www.writersbranding.com
orders@writersbranding.com

# CONTENTS

*This book is dedicated to
my daughter Lisa
for her encouragement.
Without which this book
would not have been written.
Thank you, Sweetheart.
You truly are my best friend.
I love you.*

# PROLOGUE

When his vision cleared and his thoughts came back to his head he found himself looking down at his left heel, perched on the edge of a cliff.

His vision telescoped to the waves crashing on the rocks below. His heart stumbled in his chest and beat loudly in his ears. Each beat seemed to lean him ever so slightly towards the edge. The breath froze in his lungs so suddenly that he felt dizzy. He asked himself. *How long have I been standing here?*

The only part of him that seemed to function were his eyelids. All he could do was close them and pray that this is a dream. As darkness closed on his vision, he said aloud, "Dear God help me please! Please help me!" He felt cold wind caress his back.

Being afraid that his heart and the wind would push him over the edge, he leaned back into the air. It felt like a giant pillow that touched every inch of his backside, pushing ever so gently. He was afraid to lift either foot, for fear the wind would pick him up and cast him out into the air above the ocean. He dug his heels in, leaned back and felt as if he were gently being lowered to the ground behind him. Inhaling large gulps of air he felt his heart beat throughout his whole body............ He looked! He actually opened his eyes—"Thank you. Thank you Lord. Thank you Lord", was all he could think of as he found himself on his hands and knees crawling away from the cliffs' edge. As he prayed that he had reached a safe distance he collapsed spread eagle on his stomach. With his hands and arms he gathered all the plants and soil that he could reach and hugged them tightly to his chest, curled his body around them and sobbed so deeply that his heart hurt.

# JAMES

"Hey Mister! You OK???"

He woke to a gentle poking in his ribs, unable to respond because his muscles still had him locked into a tight ball. "Mmm! Mmmm!" Was all he could manage.

"Mister!?"

Then he felt it, but could not stop what was happening to him — A hand reaching into his coat pocket. "Nnnnooo!" He managed and began to uncoil, all the while making sure that he stayed away from the cliff's edge, which when he looked, was nowhere in sight.

"No problem sir!" The young lady said. "Just trying to find some ID. Are you all right? Is there someone that I can call for you?"

He was in the middle of a park. There was a lake, he could smell it. There were evergreens, a freshly mowed lawn and a very large, wet tongue cleaning his face. For a few moments he felt like a kid again, when the family dogs' puppies would try to chew on his ears and lick his face. Rolling around on the ground, trying to get away from it, he laughed. "Nnnoo! Stop it! Ha! Ha! Stop it!"

Thinking, thinking inside his head — *is someone talking to me? — what?* Then aloud. "Who — who wants my ID?" He said as he straightened up to a sitting position, looking around again. There was a small crowd. "Oh! Man!" he said aloud and then to himself. *All these people saw me rolling around like an idiot. They'll think I'm crazy for sure?* Rubbing his head —*Who are these people and where am I anyway?* — "Where's the cliff??? It was right there," he said holding his hand out, searching for a cliff and trying to focus. Pulling it back, when he found none.

He could almost hear it again, — the voice. "Who *is* that?" he said confused. He'd been so deep in thought that his ears weren't working. There it is again.

What he heard was like someone turning the volume up and down on a radio. "—Mister! — Mister!— Mister are you OK?" Now she was shouting at him. Raising his hands to his ears to cut out some of the volume that she was producing. He nodded his head, squinted his eyes and quickly put a finger to his lips. "Shhh! Please, Mmm--my head."

"Oh! Sorry!" She said lowering her voice.

When his eyes finally re-focused, he was looking at a very beautiful woman with long, dark brown hair hanging over one shoulder. She had the face of an angel. There were baby freckles on the bridge of her cute nose, her lips opened showing perfect teeth when she said, "I'm sorry fella, but you had us pretty scared there. The way you came flying out of that van at the top of the hill and rolled all the way down here. It's a wonder that you weren't broken into little pieces," she said with concern and he noticed that she had the most beautiful chestnut brown eyes.

Coming from the people standing around, he heard:

"Do you hurt anywhere?"

"Is he bleeding?"

"Who is he? —anybody recognize him?"

"Is there somebody we can call for ya, fella?"

"George! Leave the man alone! I'm so sorry about— *George* stop! Now!" she said trying to pull the overzealous canine away. "I don't know what's gotten into him. He's *never* like this with *anyone!*"

He turned his head to see a huge, chocolate colored dog hovering over him as he sat there on the ground. He could swear that the fellow smiled at him. The dog's appearance matches his owner's chocolate brown hair and big chestnut brown eyes. The injured man wasn't sure but he thought the dog looked like a Retriever. "A Chocolate Retriever needs a Chocolate Master." he said drunkenly slurring his words. "You have pretty eyes", he said.

"Thank you! You must be an all right guy, 'cause George never smiles at anyone but me. Looks like I have some competition, here." She did a visual inspection of him and rapid fired a few questions at him to gauge his responses. "Where do you hurt? Can you stand? Can you move?" Not getting a quick response from him she called for help. "Someone help me, please. We'll put him in the shade" she said pointing in the direction of the trees. "Under the Spruce. We can get a better look at him over there."

"Mmmm! Ho— hold it he said as they tried to help him stand up. "Ohh! My head. Thank you so..... Ohh. Man! I'm really dizzy."

"Let's hurry! He'll be better lying down on the bench, than on the wet ground. Someone take his feet." she pleaded. "Please! He's not walking too well."

+++++

Again he awoke to the facial cleansing, but this time it was with alcohol and gauze. He could smell it and this time he was warm, cozy, all wrapped up and strapped to an ambulance cart. Red blue, and yellow lights flashed on every surface around him. "Wow! Man!"

A man was speaking to him, *had* been speaking to him. "—name sir? What is your name? Do you know your name?" the guy in uniform asked.

Holding up one finger he said, "How many fingers am I holding up?"

"Two?" he said with squinted eyes.

"Can you tell me your name?" He asked with concern, making notes In a little notebook.

"Yes, of course— I'm ahh!— it's— ahhh! Give me a minute!" He slurred and excitedly asked. "Where's that lady? That lady — The one that was looking in my pockets, she must have my wallet."

"That was me sir. I'm right here. Look at me, and try to focus. Hummm, your eyes are a little crossed. Your wallet must have come out of your pocket, during your roll down the hill." Sara said, "Someone should look for it."

"I've already got a couple of guys on it, Sara." An older man said. His name is Wayne Kennar, Captain of the police department here in town. He was standing by his police cruiser. The Captain is tall enough to drape his arm over the door as he keyed his microphone. Keeping the door wedged between his arm and his body he said. "Captain to Steve. You guys find anything for me?"

A static riddled voice answered back "Nothing Sir. We've covered it top to bottom. Nothing but bottle caps, empty cans and an old tennis shoe that's been here for at least a year." He paused. " — spider web inside." He confirmed by looking inside the shoe and dropping it back on the ground.

"Down what hill? Where's the cliff? Where am I?" the injured man asked urgently.

"There is no cliff sir. You're safe now. I'm taking care of you. You're at Sapphire Park. That's in Farewell, Oregon." Speaking over her shoulder, the owner of the chocolate dog said. "There's nothing in his pockets Captain. Empty. I searched him while he was passed out. I thought I could call someone for him. Only thing I found was, paper matches. I put them back. I didn't find anything written on them. The generic kind, you know plain paper cover?"

"Anybody get his name yet?" The ambulance attendant asked. "I need it for these forms." He said holding up his clipboard.

"How's about it fella, you got a name for us yet?" Sara asked. "No? Looks like it might take a while, Harry. He's got a pretty good sized goose-egg up there by his left ear and a couple more in the back."

"OK! Everybody back. Please! Give us some room." Harry instructed. "Let's get him to Dune Pines, Emergency. Sara please let the Captain know where we're taking him. I'm sure he'll have some questions for him later. Maybe have a name for ya! We'll call him James until we find out his real name." He always gave the nameless temporary identifications. A few, over the years have come back at him with, "Don't call me that. My name is Sally, Fred or whatever." Problem solved.

"Good thinking," Sara said, turned to the injured man. "If you don't mind we'll call you 'James', until we find out who ya are," she smiled waiting for his approval.

"No problem. Just don't call me late for dinner." he slurred and returned her smile.

Just as the paramedics were lifting the stretcher into the ambulance, Georges' tongue reached out and kissed the end of the injured man's nose.

"Hey Smiley! Thanks!" James said, closing his eyes, and thinking to himself. *I know, I'm going to wake-up any minute but the dog is so real. My nose is still wet— or is it? Oh! Damn my arms are strapped down. Mmmm, I don't like this. Not one bit. What the hell is my name anyway?"*

James stayed awake for the ride to the hospital. Thanks to Danny's conversation and his own racing thoughts. It was Danny's job. With a head injury he knew that it's important not to let the patient go to sleep until the doctor could take over the treatment. His mind was working overtime. They neared the ramp that took them to the emergency entrance. In fact he was nearly to a state of panic by then. He thought to himself angrily. *What's my name? What's my name? WHAT'S MY NAME, DAMN IT???* He was screaming at himself, inside his head. He was physically writhing and twisting against the safety straps. *Come on. It's right there on the tip of your tongue. Just spit it out. What's wrong with you? Damn it, come-on!*

"There, there now, take it easy son. You're breathin' too fast. Take a deep breath and hold it for a second, now let it out slowly."

James complies but it's really difficult to concentrate. His mind keeps fading in and out but he can't remember where he's been each time he comes back to where he is now. "Mmmm! This is so confusing," he said trying to put his hands up to his face.

"That's better. Don't try to sit up. We've got you strapped in so's you won't fall off while we're movin'. Just relax now. We're going to the hospital so's Doc Handle can get a look at'cha. Maybe figure out why you can't remember your name. By the way I'm Danny Coachman, volunteer fireman and, or paramedic whichever is needed."

"What happened to me?" he questioned and groaned.

"We were just coming back from taking Mrs. Henderson to the rest home, when we saw your vehicle, — Ahh! The van about two hundred yards ahead. Saw it slow down. Didn't pay much attention until you come flyin' out the side door. All curled up in a ball, you were. Just kept on rollin' right on down the hill real slow like 'cause George kept grabbin' onto you're clothes. He kept you from pickin' up too much speed on the way down. Looks like you got banged up a bit though."

"I'll have to remember to thank him. *Whoever* he is." James said.

"George? He's the dog. The one that took a fancy to ya back there in the park. I've never seen him like that around a stranger before. He kept you from rollin' all the way down the hill into the creek at the bottom. Least-wise you'd be soakin' wet and cold right now. If nobody was around you might even have drowned." Danny rambled on.

"The Dog! Oh yeah! Sure was a friendly fella. I could swear that he smiled at me. Can dogs do that?" James chuckled and smiled to himself as he remembered George—*the puppies.*

"The van didn't stop all the way. Just kind'a slowed down." Danny continued. "There was no license plate, just one of those paper advertisements. Couldn't read the name but it was red and blue letters on a white background. That should help find out who did this to you. That was *not* a friendly thing to do." Danny said sincerely, cocking his head slightly. "Got any idea who they were?"

"Naw! I can't remember who I am. I don't even remember the van that everybody keeps talking about. What is the date today?" James said closing his eyes.

"OK Danny!" Harry Sellman yelled from the drivers seat. "We're almost there so hang onto him, while I turn into the driveway. "

Danny put his hands on the railing to steady the stretcher, as the ambulance slowed to make the turn. "Today is April 1, 1995," he burst. "Ha! Some April fools day for you pal."

"You can tell whoever is in charge of jokes— this ain't funny." James said squeezing his eyes shut against the jostling pain as the ambulance maneuvered toward the double doors at the top of the emergency ramp.

"I'll have to remind the town counsel, these potholes get bigger every time it rains. Let's see how fast it gets fixed, if we have to bring one of *them* in here through that mess." Harry complained and chuckled.

# SARA & GEORGE

Dr. Lloyd Handle introduced himself. "Hi! I'm Doc Handle. Tell me! How are you feeling right now?" he asked. James replied with a troubled face while he took a mental inventory. "I feel stiff and sore, but mostly I'm confused. Can't seem to grab hold of my name even if it would save my life and this headache," he moaned closing his eyes. "You mind turning the lights down? Please! It hurts my head."

"Save your life?" Doc said dialing the lighting lower with the adjustable wall switch. "Do you know why you said that?"

"I feel the need to get away from danger of some kind. It's not far away." James answered wrapping his arms around himself, and pulling his shoulders to his ears. "When I close my eyes, I can almost see what it is, but it's around the corner. I need to hurry— run away or something. I'm really confused here."

"We're going to do everything we can to help you figure this out." Doc said. "In the meantime, let me tell you that we found nothing broken, no internal bleeding and no serious physical injury that we can see except for a few lumps on the side of your head. There's a good possibility that they caused your loss of memory. They could have happened when you came out of the van. I'm having an expert look at your x-rays tomorrow.

By then we should have your blood test results back. After I get some answers. I'll have a better idea of how to help you."

James looked down at himself for the first time, discovering that he was covered with dirt, scratches and big ugly bruises. "Mmmm!" not remembering what he looked like, he thought instantly. *This guy's been hurt. Wait a minute that's me — this is me.* He said touching his arm gingerly.

Doc saw his concern. "I'll have the ER nurse Carmine, clean those up for you. They're not serious, just uncomfortable. I'd like to keep you here until we can help you with your memory problem. This may pass in just a few days. If this turns out to be a long-term problem, there are other options. For now, we're going to think positively about this, and set a goal to cure this problem in as short of amount of time as possible. It may be as simple as a chemical imbalance, shock or an injury that needs more time to heal." Doc said as he examined inside the man's ear with a small flash light, then walked around to the other side of the bed to check the other ear. Looking into both eyes with the light before turning it off and returning it to the breast pocket of his green surgical smock. "I have no answers for you right now, so let's take this one step at a time. You and I will work on this together. OK?"

"I don't think I could ask for more than that, Doc. Sorry! Mind if I call you Doc? It seems kind'a natural to do so." James asked casually.

"Oh sure. Everybody does." Doc said. "I like it. It's informal. We'll find out more tomorrow. You just get some rest. If you have trouble sleeping let the nurse know. I'll leave a note on your chart, for something mild until we find out what's inside you already. We don't want any— bad reactions. We also need to know if you're allergic, before giving you much of anything. You just rest easy now. We'll know more in the morning."

After Carmine cleaned and bandaged the young man, she called to the two orderlies that were waiting in the hall.

They had a gurney on which to transport the patient. After they adjusted his pillow and covered him with a lightweight blanket. They took him to room 333.

+++++

"Knock! Knock! Are you decent?" It was Sara, the lady from the park.

"Decent?" James echoed. "Oh yeah! Come In!" he said motioning with his hand even though she couldn't see it through the curtain that was closed around the bed. Feeling foolish, he dropped his hand.

As she peeked around the fabric, "George wanted to come in but they wouldn't let him. He's really taken a fancy to you." She said stepping farther into the room.

"George? — Oh yeah, the dog that smiles. How could I forget," he said with his own smile. "He gives a mean bath. I'll have to remember to thank him when I get out of here." His smile turned into a look of concern by the look on her face.

"I've never seen him like this, especially with his training. I'm Sara by the way, Sara Parker," she said holding out her hand.

He took her hand, but could say nothing in return accept. "Damn, I wish whoever had my name would give it back."

"Hey! No problem. James is a cool name." She said after taking her hand back. "Can you stand up yet? Maybe you can check out the guy in the bathroom mirror. That *might* help," she said encouragingly.

"That's a good idea but I'm still hooked up to this IV. Doctor Handle said that I'm dehydrated. Man a cheeseburger and fries sound real good right about now. Better yet an inch thick porterhouse, medium rare with baked potato, sour cream and butter. Mmmm!" He closed his eyes, fantasizing.

Hey! You wan'na come back to reality here for a minute? Let's check the lap table. There should be a mirror in there." She said rolling the table closer to the bed. "Here we go, let me push it a little closer to you. There now, Just lift the table top up," she smiled encouragingly.

"Ahhh! Man this is scary! What if I don't know him, err —me?" he worried aloud. "I already don't recognize this body I'm wearing."

"Come on it can't be anything too bad, 'cause *George* likes you." She continued smiling, trying to but not too much. Just trying to keep a pleasant look on her face. To herself, she was saying *Mmm, Mmm, Mmm this guy's going to drive the nurses crazy. Good looking, with just enough ugly* to make him handsome and, his hair. Damn! What woman couldn't get lost in that long strawberry blond hair?

"OK, here it goes." He interrupted her thoughts. What he saw was totally unexpected. The guy in the mirror, needed a shave, and he saw a large bruise under his light auburn hair, all the away to below his left ear. "Wow. I'll bet that hurt, but it doesn't feel as bad as it looks," he said touching it lightly, and pulling his hand back quickly from the unfamiliar face. "As far as *who* that is — I have no idea," he said inching his head back from the reflection. "It's as if somehow, someone has changed my face,— it' all wrong." He shook his sore head in slow motion and got dizzy with the effort.

"Whose face do you think it is?" she asked with concern.

"I'm not sure of that either. No name comes to mind, but that's not how I thought I'd look." He scrunched his nose in mock disgust.

She cocked her head. "And, how do you think you *should* look?"

"I don't know for sure, just — different!! It's almost like he's the wrong guy," he said still looking in the mirror. "It's like he's the wrong nationality or something." he said closing the table mirror quickly. "It's just — Oh God! Who am I?" He said tearfully and for the second time but only the first time in his life he could remember doing so. He sobbed until his heart hurt so deeply he thought it would break. *Who am I? Where did I come from? Oh! God! Help me. I'm so lost.*

"Easy! Easy does it big fella, it's not the end of the world!" Sara said fighting back her own tears as she reached for and pressed the nurse's button. "We're going to work this out." She said as she gently rubbed his shoulder.

The nurse was there in less than a minute. "What's the problem here? Oh my! I just came on shift, I'll have to check his chart for doctors' orders." I'll be right back." She said, hurrying out of the room.

Sara continued rubbing his back consolingly. While his sobs turned to silence, his body continued quaking. Thinking *how can I help this guy? I want to help, but how? I've never actually known a person in this condition.*

The nurse returned shortly after she left. "The doctor left orders. We can give him a mild sedative." She said while swabbing his arm with alcohol then injecting the medication. "He'll be relaxing soon now."

The second nurse came in. While they both straightened his bed, and fluffed his pillow. She said. "Hey Sara. How ya doin'?"

"Fine! How's it going with you guys? I haven't seen you", *thinking it must be.* "Three weeks now isn't it? It's hard to get together now that we work different shifts." Sara told both of them as she sat in a chair beside James's bed. "I miss you guys. I loved working swing shift. I'm going to see if I can get back on it. I miss jogging with George in the mornings", she said. "Afternoon is OK but there's too much traffic. With all that exhaust, it just can't be good for you."

Crystal said, "Well! We have weekends but that's not the same as getting together *any morning* we want to."

"Maybe we should plan a picnic before the weather gets too cold," Sara added cheerfully.

Turning to James, Crystal's sister Ruby said as she lowered the head of his bed. "Is there anything else that we can do for you?"

"No. Thanks, no. I'm sorry about all the fuss," he said with an apologetic smile.

"That's not a problem!" The blond nurse said.

"It's our job." Piped in the red head. "You wouldn't want us to have nothing to do all night. Now would you?" She added with a smile that she couldn't keep off of her face.

"Thanks. You're both so kind." he said with a sleepy smile. "Thank you."

"If you need anything, just push the call button. It's clipped to your bed sheet by the pillow, right where you can reach it." The blond nurse instructed. "I'm Crystal by the way and she's Ruby."

"We have doctors orders to check on you every 30 minutes until morning." Ruby said, and the other nurse confirmed with a nod. As they left the room Crystal said, "Sara! Stop by the nurse's station before you leave. OK?"

"Will do. See ya in a few." Sara said rising from her chair. "Excuse me a minute." She stepped into the private bathroom and returned, folding a cool, damp washcloth, and said, "Here, try this." She placed the cool cloth on his forehead. "This always makes me feel better," she added.

"Mmmm! That *does* feel good," he said as she pressed the cool cloth to his head. "How can I ever repay your kindness? You and everyone I've met so far have been so kind to me. You people don't even know me."

He said sleepily as the medication started its effect. "I don't know what to say." he mumbled and then yawned. "I don't even know me." He said yawning.

"Don't say anything right now." Sara comforted "Just get some sleep. OK? I'll be by tomorrow to check on you, — if that's OK."

"That would be very kind of you to—" He drifted on his medicated cloud and smiled. He stirred a little restlessly when she pulled the cool cloth down over his eyes, and told him. "If this starts to feel a little warm, just flip it over to the cool side."

"Mmmm. This is a good thing. Thanks." He smiled. "I look forward to seeing you tomorrow."

His neck relaxed and his head turned slightly to the side. Sara knew that he slept. She silently kissed the end of her finger and ever so lightly touched it to the end of his nose. *Now why did I do that?* she smiled leaving the room quietly.

As she neared the nurses' station, Crystal said. "Sara! You're blushing. What's going on here?"

"Ahhh! He is handsome isn't he?" Ruby contributed teasingly.

"Aye! You're right about that." she smiled.

"You marked him", referring to the kiss, "didn't you?" Ruby said, more of a statement than a question.

"Yes!" She exhaled through a smile and realized that she had been holding her breath. "I couldn't help myself." She said thinking about the kiss, looking at her finger while she curled it into her palm. Looking up at the girls she said. "Lets check our calendars and get together soon OK? I really miss you guys. I've got to run, George is in the car. Let me know," she said cheerfully heading for the door.

# SECOND DAY THE
# FIRST MORNING

James was back at the cliffs edge again. It was just like the first time only he thinks, *it is* the first time. He doesn't know that he's been here before. Everything is going in slow motion. He sees — What? What is that down there? He is looking down, over the cliff. No, it's not a cliff. He's standing at the top of a very steep landslide. He would guess that it had to be at least... what sixty maybe seventy feet to the bottom? That's one that he would never try on his motorcycle. Not even on the dirt bike he just sold. He had needed the money for this trip. He couldn't bring both bikes with his and he didn't know if he would be going back to — What city was that? It seemed unimportant at the time so he just let it slide out of his mind. Telling himself that he would check it out later. The hills to steep and the dirt's too loose. Looks like it might have happened just recently. There has been a lot of rain the last few days. Shows in the soil that slid down this hill. It looks to be rocky sand, dark with rainwater. He bent over to squint at something that was sticking out of the dirt about half way down the slide area. He felt rather than saw someone take hold of his right ankle, kind of friendly. Like they were tryin' to keep him from sliding down the hill.

His eyes popped open immediately. There was a policewoman gently pressing on his right ankle. Her hair was pulled back from her face into a single braid at the back of her head. "Hello" Sara smiled at him. "How are you feeling? Do you remember me?" The hair was the color of chocolate that helped him remembered her.

"I'm feeling better than last night." James nodded slowly. "And yes I remember you but not the uniform." "Police officer! I'm impressed, if that counts."

"Yes!" She said a little too quickly and brought a pink flush to her cheeks. "It does and thank you. I was off duty yesterday. George was taking me for a walk in the park. We heard someone burning rubber up on the road just above the park. We looked up and here *you* come all curled up like a ball, rolling down the hill. George was going bonkers trying to get at you." She said with excitement, then she touted proudly. "He pulled the leash out of my hand and went after you. He was trying to grab hold of your clothing to stop your descent. He's had the training. He's a retired police officer, with three medals we keep in a drawer."

"Wow! I'm double impressed now! Congratulations to both of you.

"Double— thank you." She blushed. "I hadn't meant to brag but I love Deorge he's my Gog." She knew that she'd said it wrong and decided to let it slide. If she went back to fix it — she would draw even more attention to the verbal slip. She would turn even redder than she was already.

"The only thing I saw was the top of a white van leaving very quickly," she said recovering some of her natural color "They left a big cloud of dirt behind. That was confirmed by Danny Coachman. He's the Paramedic that rode in the ambulance with you. Said he saw the van, that pardon the pun 'dropped' you off at the park. Say! Listen! I just have a few minutes. I'm on a late lunch break."

"I'm honored. Thank you so much! That's kery vind — very kind of you," he said as the blood rushed to his entire face. "My turn." He smiled sheepishly.

They laughed together and that's what was needed to break the ice. *Silence* prevailed for a few seconds.

*Oh! Isn't that sweet.* Clearing her throat, she said: "Well, I've kept my promise to return and check on you. I try very hard not to break a promise. I've broken 3 promises in my life but this one was a breeze to keep. Hey! I see you're still sleepy. I've got to run anyway. I might stop by on my way home from work. See Ya!," she said backing out of the room.

"I'm looking forward to my second treat of the day already." He beamed at her sleepily.

*For some reason this guy makes me talk so fast I trip over my words. Didn't even give him much of a chance to answer before I almost ran out of the room. Did I? Girl Slow down will ya?* She often talked to herself stating the obvious after the fact. Not out loud but very loud inside her own head.

James slid out of bed as the door closed and made his way to the window. While standing there he noticed that this was a one-floor hospital. Constructed in a "U" shape with a beautiful miniature park in the middle. The park was filled with paved paths going in all directions, and trees with flowers planted around them. There were benches everywhere but not one person was to be seen setting on them. There was a couple of middle-aged people bundled up against the cold, fast walking in tandem together. It was getting foggy in the mini-park, the low kind that sets itself on the ground and is only about 3 feet deep. *Hmm! We must be near the water.* He thought to himself. "You can smell it," he said aloud to no one in particular for he was alone in his room. "I'm alone here! Humm! really alone. Wow! Somehow this feels— Mmm— *not* like a *bad* thing." He scanned the area outside of his window and discovered a small parking area at the inside, bottom of the "U" shaped building. The different signs posted said:

DUNE PINES HOSPITAL
FAREWELL, OREGON

AMBULANCE ENTRANCE
KEEP LANES CLEAR AT ALL TIMES

EMERGENCY PARKING
TO THE RIGHT ONLY

## VISITORS AND ALL OTHERS PLEASE PARK
## AT OR NEAR FRONT ENTRANCE

Ruby entered his room. "If you follow the yellow line on the path out there, you can go exactly one-half mile from beginning to end." Standing behind him looking out the window, she said "It crosses and goes back and forth around a few of the trees. Lots of places to sit if you get winded. Some of our staff and a few physical therapy patients enjoy it every day, weather permitting. We're supposed to have nice weather tomorrow, maybe Doc will let you sit outside in the fresh air for a while. That is if you're up to it."

"Farewell, *Oregon*???" James said as his eyes pin themselves to the sign again. "That's on the west coast, right?" he said almost absentmindedly.

"Yes!" she said, probing for a possible recalled piece of memory. "We're about 50 miles from the coast. Tell me, what are you seeing right now, in your mind? Don't think about it. Just say the first thing that comes into your mind."

Holding onto the window frame and staring at the picture in his mind, not seeing anything outside the window, he said. "I'm on my bike, a motorcycle. I'm riding along the coast, it's a beautiful day and I— I'm sca— ahh— frightened, oh man!" he inhales sharply. "I'm rushing somewhere— It's going to be too late if I don't hurry! Mmm! Nnoo!"

Ruby grabs a chair and shoves it behind his knees just as he sat rather quickly and loosely. "Hold it, hold it now! Easy does it— just sit here and hold on to the window-sill," she said as she spun and pressed the nurses call button, spun again and was holding him in the chair by his shoulders.

Crystal arrives in about seven seconds and helps her get him back into bed. She wipes his pale face with a wet washcloth, while Ruby put a call in for the doctor on duty, to come to room "333 CON. STAT." Which meant that the situation in room 333 was under *temporary* control but hurry anyway.

# THE GIFT

After breakfast he was allowed to shower. The nurse was in his room with an aid that helped her change the bed and straighten out his nightstand.

Because he wasn't too steady on his feet, he was sitting on a plastic patio chair, in the shower, under *almost* unbearably hot water. It felt so good he closed his eyes, and let the heat soak into his sore muscles. Immediately he had a vision of himself standing outside in the sunshine, —under a *hot* waterfall, surrounded on all sides by natural stone walls about thirty to fifty feet tall. The floor was a shallow pond about fifty feet across and at the deepest maybe a foot and a half. It was lined with smooth, flat, slick stones as large as two hands splayed side by side. They were of the same stone as the walls and floor accept darker because they were wet. The pond leads out to a river that was wide, cold and deep. "This is the Colorado River. I've been here. I know this place," he said out loud to himself.

Then he was back in the shower, adjusting the temperature. He washed his long hair as natural as can be. No thought to why he had hair almost long enough to reach the middle of his back. The small Band-Aids washed off of his cuts as he lathered down his lean, muscular body.

That's when he saw the tattoo on his upper arm, "Hum" and thought nothing more of it. He rinsed off and stepped out of the shower.

Wiping the mirror with the towel he stared into the stranger's eyes and asked the person looking back. "Who are you? Where did you come from? Why did someone throw you out of a van and speed away?" He looked deep into the eyes of his image. There was nothing on the surface or within that he recognized. But he knew he had to be in there somewhere 'cause he was standing there looking at this person that moved when he did. *Man! This must be the Twilight Zone or maybe I'm just one step beyond, where ever this is.* he thought, looking around the room.

He brushed his teeth, shaved and dressed in a clean hospital gown and smiled at the fact that no matter what world you're living in, hospital gowns all left you *bare assed* in the back. He grabbed the robe made out of the same material as the gown and slipped his arms into the sleeves, wincing a little at his sore muscles and bruises. Tying the belt, he left the bathroom.

"Ahh! There you are. I was going to check on you soon if you hadn't come out of there. Did you leave any hot water?" teased a young, short, blond woman that he hadn't seen before. She was probably in her early twenties by the looks of her. She had just placed his soiled sheets in a laundry cart.

"I believe so. Guess I lost track of time with my little trip down memory lane. Still don't know the guy in the mirror though." James shook his head gently. He rolled his head around to loosen the muscles in his neck.

"Oh! That reminds me. Crystal and Ruby left something for you. It's at the nurses' station, I'll be right back," she smiled and turned to leave. "Don't go anywhere," she teased as she pushed the laundry cart out of the room.

"Don't worry. I don't *want* to leave this room," he said and wondered why he was apprehensive. He caressed his forehead with all of his fingertips. He thought quietly to himself. *Why do I have this feeling of being unsafe? —*

"Here we go all wrapped up nice and here's a note to go with it." Reluctant to leave before she found out what was inside the gift. "By the way my name is Kathy, that's Kathy Manning. I'm your day nurse. If you need anything or just want to talk push my button-- ahh the nurses' button that's pinned next to your pillow," she said with a very charming flush in her cheeks. To change the subject, she said with excitement. "Are you going to open that or what? I never have been able to curb my curiosity. This is killing me!"

"Oh my! I'm sorry I was reading the note. It is very thoughtful of them but I'm curious what they mean here, look at this," he said as he handed the note to her.

*She read it out loud:*

*Good morning! -*

*We, (Crystal and I) were thinking that maybe this small gift will be of some use to you while you're trying to gather your lost thoughts. Sometimes the mind has many locked doors and we would like to help you find the keys, if you will let us.*

*We get special vibrations that you are a good person, but you are (obviously) very troubled. See you tonight when we come on duty.*

*Ruby and Crystal Smith*

"OK let's see what this gift is and maybe we can figure it out," she said while he unwrapped it.

"It's a small notebook. Leather bound," he announced. "This is really nice. It has a pen and mechanical pencil set. Here." he said handing the book to her. "Check it out, what do you think? I'm about as curious as you were *before* I unwrapped it."

"Oh, I get it," she said as she thumbed through the blank pages. "They did this before, with a little boy that was hit in the head with a baseball at his little league game."

"Poor little guy couldn't remember a thing. Not even his folks." He couldn't write very well but he was a good artist. Filled that little book with lots of pictures. They had him look at every page before he went to sleep at night. In three days, he was back on track, asking his Mom and Dad to take him home 'cause he was tired of hospital food. They scooped him up and headed for the door as soon as Doc Handle gave his OK.

"That's probably what they're thinking about you. You could write everything down that comes back to your memory, or questions you might have. You read it all every night before you go to sleep." Kathy said triumphantly. "It might help. Give it a try. Who knows?" she said handing the notebook back to him.

"Right now -- I'll try anything," he said, as he absent-mindedly kept clicking the mechanical pencil until the lead popped out of the end, landing on his lap. "Oh my!" He clicked it again until just a small amount of lead showed at the tip.

"Well, it looks like you've found something to write, so I'll be on my way" Kathy said as she turned on one foot toward the door.

"Hey! Wait!" He said, stopping her in mid-stride. "What's that about the 'vibrations' part? Are they psychic or something?" He asked with concern.

"As a matter of fact. Yes, they are. Quite good too. They're twins. Not identical but twin just the same. Kind of spooky in a way. There are people that want to study them, but they won't have anything to do with it. They say, 'We have something special and we don't want anybody mucking it up.' I can understand that." Kathy said as she eased herself down on the edge of the bed. "They have always worked the same shift together, go shopping together, everywhere you see one, just look around and you'll find the other not far away. They even double date; it drives the guys bonkers."

"Oh!" She blushed, [The staff are not supposed to sit on the patient's bed.] standing quickly and turned to straightening the blanket where she had been sitting. "Sorry! — I've got to get back to work. See you with your lunch tray." She said as she reluctantly left this beautiful man's room.

As he watched her leave, he fingered the notebook and clicked another piece of lead onto his lap. "Oh! Man! What's happening here?"

Eyeing the book, he clicked twice more and proceeded to open it to the first page, thinking to himself, "What do I remember? Nothing!" He shuddered, and felt like the blank page he was looking at. "No! That's not true. No! Stop it!" He chided himself. *You'll get nowhere thinking like that. Come on now let's do this.* He proceeded to write one word on each page, then he could add to each as the words conjured pictures in his mind. When he finished with what memory allowed, he reviewed the pages.

So far he had:
Motorcycle - Honda 500 - where is it? On beach / over cliff.
Had a dirt bike sold it - $ for the trip I'm on. Where from?
Feeling - too late if I don't hurry.

Tattoo - upper left arm - single rose - no name.

Hot springs - waterfall - Colorado River? Arizona?

Cliff - above ocean - cliffs' edge crumbled down to
the shore, like it fell away in an avalanche -
very steep - looked fresh.

Heel on edge, almost fell over. Very frightened.
Last memory before park.
What happened before park?
George and Sara.

Where is that cliff????????

White van - not a memory - was told.

He closed the book and leaned his head back against the pillow. "Oh man! This headache!"

+++++

"Still at it I see." Kathy said as she entered James' room. "That was a good idea." she said pointing her nose at the book because her hands were holding his food tray. "Here's your lunch. We've got a new cook; this looks pretty good. Some of the staff has started eating in the cafeteria again, including myself. Here! — You need to get back in bed, you're looking a little pale," she said as she pushed the control and raised the head of his bed. "I'll move your lap table in front of you, so you can relax while eating this delicious lunch. Mmm! Smells good. Looks like Italian today. I know where I'm eating lunch," she said, lifting the plate cover. Remember, if you need anything—."

"I know, *just push your button.*" He said teasingly.

"Yes," she blushed again and spun to leave the room, clearing her throat as she went through the door.

*Too sweet and too young. Almost painfully cheerful.* He thought to himself. *Maybe it just bothers me 'cause I'm not feeling too good yet. Man, this headache— thinking too hard, I guess.* Sucking in his breath, he said aloud. "It can wait, I'm not ready to push the panic — nurses' button yet." *Probably should eat something, I am hungry.* Taking the first bite, "Mmmm" He smiled loudly around a mouth full of food that was delicious. "Good stuff." He proclaimed aloud. He didn't finish lunch. He fell asleep while eating.

# CAPTAIN KENNAR

James woke up from his nap to find his lunch tray still in front of him. His sleep had produced no dreams this time. He felt pretty good, relaxed and hungry again. He closed his eyes, stretched, turned over, opened one eye and looked right into Captain's smiling face.

Wayne Kennar is fifty-seven years old, five foot nine inches, and two hundred thirty-five pounds. Salt and pepper brown hair and not very much salt, and he has a robust muscular build. He transferred to Farewell, Oregon to replace the retiring Captain. His last job was Sergeant on the force in a region of Alaska, eight years ago. As he approached his fiftieth birthday, he decided that Alaska wasn't for him. *Too cold for these old bones*, and besides wife and fifteen-year-old daughter were gettin' distressed and wanted to leave all this ice and snow behind. They wanted rain that didn't freeze, green trees, and winters that were not mostly dark. Jill told her father more than once, that she was growing mold 'cause there wasn't enough sunshine. Janet, his wife and he had agreed that it was time to move south towards the sunshine. It wasn't two weeks later that the opportunity came to move here to Farewell. Wayne's Uncle was retiring the post and wanted to know if he could talk Wayne into coming here to take his place. The town council had already given him free reign to choose his successor. Why not have another Kennar sitting in the Captain's chair. Won't even have to change the name on the door.

Three weeks later he moved his family and all their belongings to Farewell.

+ + + + +

The Captain was out of uniform, dressed in Levi's and a sweatshirt with a picture of Daffy Duck on the front. Actually, it was just a pair of eyes and a large orange duckbill on solid black, that couldn't represent any other character than Daffy, himself.

James liked him right off, it takes a certain kind of guy to wear a shirt like that and look like he'd punch anybody out that thought he shouldn't. He couldn't speak yet, but kept his one open eye on Daffy while he collected his thoughts, all he could do was smile sleepily and raised his eyebrows. "Mmm hello Daffy."

"Hi there! You cleaned up pretty good!" Wayne said cheerfully. "You look a lot different than you did last night." He waited a short time, letting the young man collect his wits, and stuck out his hand and said. "My name is Wayne Kennar. Captain Wayne Kennar of the police department here in Farewell. That's in Oregon in case nobody's told you yet."

"Mmm yeah! I saw it through the window, - - - the sign in the parking lot." James said, poking his hand out to shake the Captains hand. With his sore muscles preventing him from sitting up without a struggle, he pushes the button to raise the head of his bed. "Sorry I haven't got a name for you yet. They're calling me 'James' for now. I don't mind, it's better than 'hey you' or 'what's his names' isn't it?" He smiled.

"Don't push it and maybe it will come around a little easier. Sometimes if you try too hard, it makes it more difficult. Relax! Please understand, we're not pushing you. I stopped by to see if I could be of any help. I'd like to fingerprint you if you don't mind. Maybe it could speed things up a bit. How do you feel about it, any problems there?" Wayne asked.

"Well— I'm not sure. I felt a little apprehensive, when you said 'fingerprint'. Maybe it's excitement, I don't know— something inside me is saying 'no,' but let's just do it. How long will it take to find out who I am?, James asked.

Wayne shrugged "Can't be sure. It depends. Normally not too long. Then again if you're in the witness protection program" He paused. "Well, let's cross that bridge *only* if we have to. I'll send one of my lab guys over later. "Have you got any other concerns, or questions while I'm here? Anything? Guy stuff, you don't feel you can ask your nurse?"

"Now that you ask—" James said quietly as he leaned forward a little. "Yes! I'm rather lost here; I don't know anybody. I don't have one item that belongs to me. I don't have two coins to rub together and I'm dying for a Pepsi. The clothes I had on were trashed. I don't know if I can pay the hospital bill, it must be a fortune by now. Where am I going to stay when I get out of here? I'd like to have some underwear, and street clothes, is there a Good Will around here? Maybe I could trade some labor for some food and clothes— and— Oh! God what's happening to me?" He started speaking more rapidly. "Why do I feel so frightened when I think of leaving here. I'm. I'm OH! God, Please!!!" He was breathing hard, sweating and getting very wide-eyed.

As he reached for the nurses button Wayne said. "Hey! Hey! Easy big fella! Let's slow it down a bit now." Wayne added as he patted James on his shoulder. "We'll take this one step at a time. You just lay back now and take some slow breaths. That's right, sloowww, deeeep, that's better, a little slower, relax now. I know you want all the answers now but that doesn't look like it's going to happen."

As the nurse entered the room, Wayne said, "Sorry, I had no idea he was wound up so tight, I guess I should have expected it. I know I'd be freaked out if I woke up in another world." The nurse was prepared for what was needed. She had a small tray in her hand with his medication already in a syringe. She swabbed his arm with alcohol, and gave him an injection. "This is mild but it will calm him down," she said lowering the head of his bed, straightened his bed sheets and then left the room with a smile.

"I'm sorry! It's just that I can't remember depending on anyone before, I feel like I've always been independent. Now I've lost control of my entire life. Who the hell am I?, What's my name, and where did I come from? Why— am I so frightened." He sat up leaning forward as he wiped his sweaty brow with the back of his hand.

Wayne gave James a fatherly pat on the back and said "Leave all those questions to me right now son. That's my job. We'll take things one at a time until we get from the bottom to the top of this. OK? Now you just get some rest and let your body heal first, then we'll figure it out together, OK?" I'm gonna let you rest now. I'll see you tomorrow.

"Before you leave, take a look at this," James said and handed Wayne the notebook. "This is the total sum of my knowledge as of this minute, film at eleven."

"Ahh! I see the Smith twins are aware of your problem. This is very good news. Consider it a good omen, son. These ladies know their stuff. They don't help just anybody either. I see by the note folded inside here that they are volunteering to help you without you even asking for help. That's a *very* good sign young man."

"Yes. Kathy Manning told me about them this morning. I started writing as soon as I was alone. I didn't find much to write about, but check out what I've got so far."

"OK, this is interesting. Mind if I copy these down into my notebook?" Wayne asked, as he pulled out his own notebook.

"No, not at all. My hope, is that you can get something from such a small list," James said hopelessly.

"Fear not young man. 'Small maps, find big treasures." Wayne recited as he flipped open his own leather-bound notebook. It was small enough to fit in his shirt pocket. He copied the young man's list, looked up and saw him watching the procedure. "Yes, I've carried one of these, since I met the twins. Almost seven years ago now. Never leave home without it, keep it with my keys and grab it on the way out the door. Personal stuff mostly, I start a new one every year, on my birthday. Ahh! — The trips I've had down memory lane, just thumbing through the old ones. Someday I'll pick this one up and think to myself, '*Ahh! What a grand time we had back then. He said* almost dreamily under the influence of past memories. He cleared his throat and finished copying what he needed and handed the other notebook back to the young man. "I'm going to get right on this," he said placing the chair back where he had found it against the wall. "See ya later." As he reached the door, he turned. "You just relax and let me see what I can come up with. Get some rest now. OK? I left my card on your table there, if you remember anything else, *please* feel free to call. If I'm not in the office, someone will know where I am." Anxious to get started, he said "good-bye" and hurried to the parking lot.

After Wayne left James put his head back on the pillow and drifted lazily on the mildly pleasant current of the drugs the nurse had administered to him. He couldn't remember why he was so upset.

# SHARING

"Mmm! Something smells good." James mumbled to himself as he opened one eye, to see Crystal setting his dinner tray on the lap table, pushing the lunch tray off to the side with the tray she was holding. He hadn't eaten much. She removed the plate cover and was fanning the delicious smells in his direction, and smiling mischievously.

"Before you look, tell me what's for dinner," Crystal said, shielding the plate from his view.

"Thanksgiving dinner, with all the trimmings," he said hungrily rubbing his hands together.

"Close your eyes before you tell me," Crystal instructed. "That's right. Sit up a little straighter, now slowly and deeply, breathe in through your nose and exhale the same way through your mouth. That's good. Now see if you can do this without making any breathing sounds," she said quietly and almost whispering.

"Roast beef with— with potato wedges and whole carrots baked in the juice," he said enthusiastically as his eyes popped open.

"Excellent! You want the stuffed animal or the dinner??" She asked teasingly, holding the tray just out of his reach.

"I think I could eat both as hungry as I am. That's a neat trick, can you teach me any others? You're Crystal, right?" He said, reaching for the tray.

"Right. It's Crystal. Actually, Ruby is better with the tricks than I am." She said picking up the lunch tray. "Do you want this apple from your lunch tray?" she asked. "Maybe for a mid-night snack? You might get hungry; it looks like you slept right through lunch."

"Good idea!," he said reaching for the fruit. Then pointing to the lunch tray, he said smiling widely. "Could you please put that Jell-O in the refrigerator for me? Purdee please???"

"Not a problem." She smiled and turned to leave to room. "We'll be back to check on you later," she called over her shoulder. "Enjoy dinner!"

He fell asleep almost as soon as he finished dinner and awoke to the blood pressure cuff being squeezed onto his left arm. He still had the spoon in his right hand. "Ahh Mmmm!" he said as he sucked his breath in with a hiss.

"Sorry." Ruby said apologetically. "There's not a place on you that's not been banged-up, bent or scratched. I'll hurry, I've almost got it."

"Those things hurt anyway." Crystal said holding out her hand for the spoon, before taking the tray away.

"Thank you, ladies, for the notebook with the fancy pen and pencil set. That was very kind of you both. I didn't understand at first, but Kathy told me about the little boy that you helped. I didn't draw any pictures, but I wrote a few things in it. Here! You wan'na take a look? This is all I could think of till now," he said, holding the notebook out to them.

Ruby took it and handed it to her sister after she got rid of the tray. Without opening it, she pressed it between both of her flattened palms (like praying). Closing her eyes as she held it up and touched the corner of the book to her forehead and touched the bridge of her nose with both thumbs. Her eyes snapped open and she was looking directly at him. "Does the name Carl mean anything to you? Maybe anything about a bridge?" She started to tremble.

"Mmm, no not really," he said with a thoughtful shrug of his shoulders.

Ruby walked over and placed her hand on Crystal's hands. She was still holding the book to her forehead and trembling. She pulled them away from her sister's face and looked into her eyes and spoke. "That was fast this time. Perhaps we can get more details later."

"He wrote it in pencil," Crystal added, still holding the notebook.

"That's good." Ruby said looking at James.

"Why is that?" He said with curiosity.

"Pencil is changeable, flexible, and erasable. Ink is, stationary, ridged and permanent. The choice was up to you," Ruby told him.

Clearing his throat, he said. "I didn't know I had a choice. I just picked up the pencil absentmindedly. Wow! Did I just say *absent mind*? 'HA!'" He burst.

Dismissing the pun Ruby said. "You think it was a mindless choice, but I assure you it wasn't. We'll talk more about *that* later. Time permitting," she said holding out a hand as Crystal offered her the book.

"The *paranormal* has always fascinated me," he offered.

"Now, let's see what you've got written in here. This tells me you're an organized person. This is probably why Crystal was able to scan it so quickly. Look at this Sissy, he's got one item on each page, leaving room for after thoughts."

"Your motorcycle will be found soon if it hasn't already. You'll have to fix it up before you ride it again. You had a passenger the last time you rode it," Ruby frowned. "She's not clear to me yet. I'll have to come back to her later. Her aura didn't influence yours at all. It's like her aura was a very weak to begin with or she didn't have one, which is only possible if you're dead. But she couldn't have been riding a motorcycle if she was dead, now could she?"

"That really puzzles me," he offered.

"The tattoo is a name— it is 'Rose', in memory of your twin sister." She continued, "I see she was a large part of your life up until recently. The artwork in your skin is a physical bond and a focal point for your spiritual connection with Rose. That was not severed by her death. Your spirits are still connected and will always be. Your connection will be reestablished with the dissipation of the wall. Maybe someday you'll let us meet her spirit."

"It may help to think of this wall as being like *writer's block*, with all the information in there just waiting for the wall to come down." She paused looking at him.

"I get a good feeling from the waterfall." The twins - both smiled.

"I remembered that one in the shower this morning," he offered.

She continued with a quick look in his direction for the interruption. "Bats and mosquitoes when the sun goes down." Ruby cringed and spoke. "I believe we've been there, Sissy. It's up the river about 30 minutes from Willow Beach. You're right, it is the Colorado River. The only way to get there is by boat. You pull into this little alcove and tie the boat so the river won't pull it out on its strong currents. It's very secluded. You walk between rock walls, down a short passage, then voila you're in a small enclosure with a naturally heated waterfall."

The twins smiled at each other. He could tell they were sharing a picture in their minds. He wanted to be at the waterfall with them. They both turned to look at him, — instantly — they were sharing the warm waterfall together. Then after a few moments he was back in the room, right where he was a minute ago.

"WOW! That was *nice*. Thank you so very much! I'll never forget this experience ladies." He said astonished that he wasn't wet. "Hey! I remember that place. I was there with a friend and her two kids. Her little girl got stung because the 'yellow jackets' were attracted to the glow sticks we were using for light."

*Glow stick: A flexible clear plastic tube with a sealed capsule inside. When you bend the plastic tube and break the little capsule inside, the chemicals mix and produce a bright light, often used instead of a flashlight or a lantern.*

"It wasn't just us that got you there." They told him. "Your desire was so strong, we decided to take you along. You needed this experience to strengthen your confidence in us. If you do not trust us completely, if you put up confinements, then we cannot help you at all." Ruby admonished.

"If you speak of this to anyone, we will deny it, because they'll come get us. They already want to dissect our brains, trying to see if they can duplicate what we do. We've already got people bugging us about it."

"Mums the word ladies. You just confirmed to me that paranormal things are real. That was beautiful. Thanks, again." He gushed with excitement.

"You're the first one we've ever shared with. If you were to ask me why, I could only tell you that it felt like the right thing to do." Ruby said.

Still holding the book Ruby said, "Your cliff experience was most difficult for you. You probably think it's around here, but the closest cliffs are fifty miles west, — on the coast. I believe your bike will be found on the coast."

"The white van was — I don't see ownership — might be brand new, probably from a dealership. It's still out there. Hasn't been returned. Wayne needs to know this. We'll see you later, we need to make a phone call." Leaving the book on the table, both women left the room.

# THE PARK

This was exciting. He couldn't get himself to relax. He got out of bed after about five minutes and slipped into his robe tying the belt and stepped into the hospital slippers. He walked to the nurse's station down the hall. The twins were there, "Do ya think I could wander around for a while? I'm still kind'a wound up a little." He asked nicely.

"Oh, sure that's not a problem. Why don't I give you the tour? Ruby's waiting for a phone call, and our patients are not allowed to roam without an escort." Crystal informed.

"I'm not feeling like much of a tourist. Do you mind if we sit in the little park I've been admiring outside my window? It's the fresh air, I think I need." He begged with one raised eyebrow and a smile.

"That sounds like a good idea." Crystal said, tapping Ruby on the shoulder giving her a 'twin signal'. (Not all, but some twins have their own, private way of communicating.) Carl understood saying nothing. Those kinds of things were personal and he was unwilling to interrupt. *Maybe later.*

Ruby nodded and continued with some patient charts that were on the desk.

"Let's stop at the soda machine before we step outside. I'm buying." Crystal said while fishing for change in her uniform pocket.

"O.K.! Thanks! Soda sounds good right now. You guys are being really nice." He said pulling his shoulders up to his ears.

"My pleasure. You first." She said while inserting some change into the machine. He pushed the only Pepsi button and he heard the cans rolling around inside the machine. "Ka-thud! Ka-Plop!" Out pops two Pepsi's. "Oh my!" She said a bit flustered. "Oh! This kind of thing happens when I get excited. One time I got about seven soda cans at one time out of a machine at the Mall. This boy I had a crush on, stopped to talk with me while I was getting a soda. This time it's because it's the first time I've shared a *three-way* vision with anybody. That was quite a thrill for me. It's usually just the two of us, my sister and I before today. I didn't know we could." She said rapidly while fumbling to get the two cans out of the machine. She straightened up, holding one can in each hand and said with a gesture of her head. 'Follow me.' They stepped outside of the air-controlled building. "This is nice. A bit cool but very nice. It smells so good out here. Maybe I work outside for a living? My skin looks to be tanned." He said popping open the top of his soda as they walked across the two-lane paved road into the little park. He held out his empty hand for her inspection. "I have calluses on my hands.

"Perhaps. You could have gotten those riding your motorcycle. With no tan-line on your wrists, you don't wear gloves." She said looking around a little apprehensively. This wasn't the first time that she'd brought a patient outside of the building but she felt a little uneasy about it today.

"Humm! That makes sense too." He said inspecting his hands again. "I hadn't thought of that. Ruby said something about my having a passenger the last time I rode my bike. That bothers me, because —" He paused thinking and continued more or less thinking out loud. "because if I came out of the accident this bad. What about — them or whatever happened to me, or us. I'm confused. I don't know how to feel about this whole situation. I can't help but wonder. What happened to my passenger and what happened to my motorcycle?" He questioned without expecting an answer.

They spotted a couple benches and sat down next to one of the many picnic tables.

"I'm positive that Captain Kennar will find out something soon. Let me assure you that he is very good at his job." she said. "We'll also have your blood test result back tomorrow. They'll help the doctor help you." She reassured him. "It seems we have company." she said looking over his shoulder, as the patrol car turned into the entrance and headed in their direction.

"I'm glad I spotted you." Wayne shouted as he finished rolling the car's window down. "I'll park in the lot and be right with you."

Crystal said, "See! Here comes some news already." They stood and walked toward the parking area, both anxious to hear any news at all.

Wayne said, "I've had some of my information requests returned with answers. It's not *all* good. Let's find a table." It was only a few feet to a small table and chairs where they made themselves comfortable.

"First of all." Wayne set his briefcase on the table. "A motorcycle was found about half way to the bottom of a rather steep land slide. It's about seventy-five feet down to the beach. From the looks of it, the bike took the turn too fast, laid down and slid to the edge. The soil was saturated, due to a recent rain they had. It crumbled pretty easily. The weight of the bike took a good chunk of earth with it."

Some folks walking on the beach, yesterday morning, reported it. They saw the handlebars and part of a front tire sticking out from under the sand and soil in the slide area.

When the tow truck pulled it out, there was a young woman or rather teenage girl strapped to the backrest. The coroner, said she's about 16 years old. He also says she'd been dead about 12 hours before she got buried with the bike. Obviously, a drug overdose, she'd been molested sexually, and beaten pretty badly. She had a broken neck, but that happened hours before she went over the cliff. They've started a review of missing person's reports trying to match her description. We should know more by tomorrow." Wayne explained.

The FBI is anxious to talk to you because one of the drugs in the girl, matches with a drug that was taken in a robbery last week. They're curious to find out what drugs show up in your blood tests, as well. I told them that you have amnesia and are unaware of your own name. That'll hold them for a short time at least. We're going to step up our efforts and maybe get the answers we need, while we've still got the FBI at arm's length. I can't believe they'll give us much time.

"The Bike is registered to a 'Carlton F. Bridgeman, of Manhattan Beach, California.' Does any of this ring a bell with you?"

Crystal and James looked at each other and James said, pointing at her. "Crystal, didn't you ask me earlier if the name *Carl* meant anything to me, or something about a *bridge*?

She silently replied with a nod.

"Say!!! You're good!" He smiled and drank about half his Pepsi down in one double gulp. Good or bad, any news was exciting to James. "I don't know about 'Carlton' but 'Carl' fits really good on my tongue, — like I've said it a lot. I also have another request— Can we please change James, to Jim. James sounds a little stuck-up to me. I don't feel anything like a 'James — James Bond' that is. It's the same with Carlton, if that turns out to be my name. I just know I'd like Carl better. Carlton would be like what — a butler?" "Ha!" he hooted, messaged his forehead and sighed "Oh man!"

"That's O.K. son we'll figure this out. Leave this to *me* and you spend *your* time getting well." He couldn't help himself; he liked this young man.

"The only memory that I have of being on my bike, was that I was scared, and I had to hurry somewhere, or it would be too late."

Captain Kennar asked the obvious questions. "Have any idea of why it was going to be *too late*, or maybe *what* you are frightened of?"

Jim shook his head. "No Sir. I'm still in the fog on a lot of things and I don't remember a passenger. Seems like a passenger would be holding on to me." He said and his mind went into— nothing, he could not conjure a picture of her in his mind.

Crystal interrupted "They said that the girl was tied to the bike."

"That brings two questions to mind right off." Jim said. "Was she unconscious? And if not, why was she tied to the bike. I can't picture anyone wanting a seatbelt on a motorcycle."

Crystal informed Wayne of Ruby's and her plan to talk with James after they get everybody else settled in for the night.

"That's good. If anybody can speed up the recovery of his memory you two can." Captain Kennar said as he stood up offering his hand to the young man without a name. They shook hands and the captain said, "I'll come by again tomorrow. Right now, I've got to get home and feed Samson, my dog. He lets me know if I'm late too. He greets me, and then follows me around with his food dish clamped in his jaw, until I kick off my shoes and lock my gun up. He's a pest but I wouldn't trade him for anything. We're pals he and I. Good night son. See ya tomorrow Crystal.

Without warning Crystal shivered and knew that danger was near.

"Good evening Wayne," she replied as she also stood, almost urgently tugging on Jim's elbow. "Come on. We should head back in. The ground fog is coming in. We don't need you getting a chill." She said as she hurried him towards the Hospital doors.

They didn't see the pickup truck that cruised by just after the double doors shut behind them.

The driver didn't see *them* either.

The hospital doors and windows were the kind that you can't see through from outside, they look to be made of black glass. You can see out but not in. It's the same kind of glass you see in office building, they reflect your image like a mirror.

# CLOSE CALL

It took only a minute, for Wayne to get to his cruiser to call headquarters telling them that he was on his way back to the station. By the time he was in motion, he found himself slowed down by a pickup truck that was leaving the lot. He said out load to himself admiringly "Hmm! Nice truck. Owner takes good care of it. What is that about a 53?" and as it turned left, out onto the street. "Step side too — nice!"

Nurse and patient had entered the building by the time he drove by.

Wayne turned right, and as he headed for the station, he thought out loud. "I don't usually think much of long hairs, but I really like this guy. There's just something about him— I don't know what it is— And, what about the way George took to him? — I hope he's not a disappointment, maybe mixed up with that dead girl."

An image of Ruby flashed across his mind's eye as he picked up the radio microphone. She often reaches out to Wayne in this manner. *That reminds me*— he thought. After his call was answered he said aloud. "This is the Captain again Jill. When the Night Sergeant comes in, have him send a man over to guard room 333 at Dune Pines Hospital. He's the guy that was dropped off at the park. Let's make sure that he doesn't get thrown down anymore hills."

"Aye! Captain - I'll tell him right now, he just walked in. — Anything else Sir?" Jill asked.

"Just one! Call Ruby Smith at Dune Pines and tell her I'll call her as soon as I get home." Then he added, "You'll be off of your shift when I get back, so have a good evening. See you tomorrow, he signed off with a smile.

Jill grinned. "Good night Dad!"

+++++

When Wayne got home, Samson was waiting with his plastic bowl locked in his jaw. "Hi there, fella! What-cha been doin' all day besides sleeping?"

Samson's tail was wagging so fast, his back paws were sliding back and forth, dancing little circles on the linoleum floor.

He finished putting his gun away, getting out of uniform and taking care of Samson. In the kitchen he grabbed a cold beer and string cheese out of the refrigerator, some chips off of the top and headed for the sofa. He called Ruby at Dune Pines. "East Wing please." He said and used the remote control to turn the television on, while he waited.

Ruby was on the phone in less than a minute. "East wing, Ruby speaking.

"This is Wayne. Got your message. Your image gets stronger all the time. Maybe someday I won't have to call you to find out what you want. Keep practicing. What's up young lady?"

"More like you've got to practice receiving big fella. She bantered in their usual friendly tone. We should set some practice time aside.

Maybe you *did* get my message. It's already taken care of. One of your guys— 'Justin Walker' just showed up for guard duty. I was getting a little antsy. After all, somebody did hurt this guy pretty bad. I was thinking that maybe they might know where he is. I had a *real strong* feeling of apprehension, right after Crystal brought her patient back inside the building. She was aware of it too. She rushed him back in the building right after you left. I also see color — turquoise around or near him. "I think that we should keep him inside, until we know more about him or his enemies."

"Yeah. We don't want him running off by himself either." Wayne added. "If the wrong person does know where he is. — We should know more details by tomorrow. Good luck, tonight— when you visit with him. You know where I'm at if anything important comes up. Good night.

"We'll go easy on him. It hasn't even been thirty-six hours, since they brought him in. Good night, Wayne," she said hanging up the phone.

+++++

When Jim got back to his room, the finger print technician was just seating himself in a chair, preparing to await Jim's return. His bottom end didn't touch the chair for three seconds when he returned to a standing position. "Hello, I'm here from the police department lab services. My name is Alfred Chase and this is my witness Crystal Smith, she will verify that you are the person belonging to the fingerprints I'll be taking here today, or rather this evening." Clearing his throat politely and holding up his hand in a request for silence he said, "I realize that you *already* know your nurse, but I had to make it *official* with an introduction. I need a witness, because you do *not* remember your name. Do you have any questions before I get started?"

"No! Lets' do this. I'm anxious to find out who I am" Jim said excitedly, and added with a wink in Crystal's direction. "I had the feeling that they were going to start calling me 'John Doe' or something else equally as dull or non-descript."

After the print technician left his room, Jim washed his hands and climbed back into bed to take a nap. His muscles were sore, but he didn't want any more drugs so he closed his eyes and tried to relax. The next thing he knew — he was drifting.

+++++

He's looking down again but not at the cliff, this time. This time he's looking down the end of a pool stick. He sees money laying on the side of the pool table. Looking a little higher, beyond the table, he sees a girl. This time he looks closer. She is leaning back, with her head on the wall behind her in the corner. Even with those big sunglasses on he can tell that she's young. And too much make-up. She probably thinks they'll hide her age. What is she doing with these guys anyway? *Kids these days. Probably a runaway.* He thought to himself. *She doesn't look like she feels well, probably drunk, with her arm hanging down like that. Her legs spread apart. Not very lady like of her. Yeah, she's probably passed out. She's going to have quite a hangover in the morning. Leave it alone. She isn't your problem.* Now someone's trying to take the pool stick out of his hand. "It's still my turn." He shouted as his eyes popped open.

It was Ruby trying to get him to let go of the bed railing. "Shhh! Now it's not always your turn. I need your arm for a few minutes, so I can take your blood pressure then I'll give it right back. O.K.? She said with a teasing smile.

"Mmmm! Sorry! Sure go ahead." He looked at Ruby a little confused as he relaxed his arm.

"Your heart is really racing. You have a bad dream?" Ruby asked concerned.

"I can't say if it was a bad dream or not. I believe it was a memory, more than a dream. It was so realistic, the details." He told them of what he saw, the girl and everything else he just experienced.

Ruby and Crystal both agreed that they would leave the room while he wrote everything in his notebook, just as he remembered it from his dream. Else he would be distracted and forget the details, or get confused. They left saying that they would return when he pressed his call button.

Please take your time. We'll be here all night." Whispered Crystal.

To the notebook he added:
Playing pool / location unknown
I see money laying on the side of the pool table.
Girl with big sunglasses - can tell that she's young.
She doesn't look well — probably drunk, arm hanging down -
legs spread apart, not very lady-like of her, probably passed out.

As he finished writing, he pressed the calling button. While he waited, he absent-mindedly picked up the apple from his table and munched hungrily, sucking loudly at the juice that threatened to drip down his chin with each bite. As he was reaching for the box of tissues for his sticky hands, the twins appeared in the doorway, smiling.

Crystal said, "I believe your wash-cloth is still damp, it will work better on sticky hands. The tissue will stick to your fingers." She caught a question that came from his eyes, and said, "Yes that's why some say a thief has sticky fingers. Just about anything he wants sticks to his fingers, or hers, depending—."

"That's spooky!" he said aloud. "You heard my question and answered before I could say anything."

"Sorry, I didn't mean to intrude on your thoughts, but you're projecting so strongly." Crystal said in astonishment. "Please be assured that we can only read what's projected to the surface of your mind. We cannot read your private thoughts." She said reassuringly. "Please believe me. Don't turn away from us because you think we can read all of your thoughts. Some people refuse to be in the same room with us, because of their fear."

"I have no reason to believe, or disbelieve you." He said, as he looked into her eyes with honesty. "I don't fear you or your sister. I get a peaceful feeling, coming from you both. And, I can't believe I just said that. What's happening here? I don't understand what's going on?" He asked, confused yet excitedly.

"This is what we do." Ruby said. "If you are uncomfortable, we'll stop right now. Just say the word. We just thought it would be best to introduce our methods to you while you were in a relaxed state of mind, like now when you're just waking up. It cuts down on the fear factor. Fear can put on the brakes sometimes. It's impossible to help a person while fear is controlling them."

Bowing and shaking her head Crystal interjected. "People that have too much fear." She said looking into her private space for a few seconds. "It's sad."

Ruby said, "Actually it's more like *you*, tapped into *us*. Your signal is strong right now, but it may fade as you heal and the foreign drugs leave your system. You have a strained aura around you. We have seen this with amnesia patient before." she informed him, and then added. "This is taking a lot of energy, we can talk more later," she and Ruby pulled their energy back, exhaling with tired relief.

He felt the disconnection immediately, almost like having his brain switch turned from high to medium. "WOW! What a rush, going from one level to the other," he said holding the railing as if he would fall out of bed. "When can we go again? I feel great."

"Mmmm, you sound like you're going to be very disappointed when this fades away. Please don't get your hopes up, too high. You may find yourself in a depression that could be emotionally painful." Ruby warned.

"Yes ma'am! I already *am*, disappointed." He said with a small salute and a smile, "but I understand what you're saying. 'When the rides over, you got'ta get out of the car.' Humm! Somebody used to say that, a lot. I wonder who?" he pondered.

"Well." Crystal interjected, with a faux French accent, and winked teasingly. "You aren't ze only guest we have here at Chez Dune Pines, and ze other two nurses will be needing our help as soon as the doctors finish with the two emergencies that came in a while ago. Would you like ze Jell-O from your lunch before we get *too busy* to *bozier* with you?" She continued with a big smile, letting him know, she was kidding about being *too busy* to *bother*.

"That would be a treat, thanks," he said aloud, then thought to himself. *Nice young lady so thoughtful.*

"Yes, she is. Thank you." Ruby said as she and her sister left the room.

Crystal was back quickly. "Here's your Jell-O," she said setting it down with a plastic spoon and napkin. Then checked to make sure that his pillow was fluffed and he had fresh water for the evening. "Do you need anything else, before I go back to some real work?" She chided cheerfully.

"I'm getting another headache; do you think that I could get something for the pain?" He asked, pinching the bridge of his nose.

"Sure! Why don't you settled in for the night, I'll be right back" Crystal said as she left the room.

As he leaned back on the pillow, he turned the television to the cartoon channel, with the remote control.

"You *must* know that too much education will make the brain swell." Doc Handle said, stepping into the room wearing his green surgery garb with a green mask hanging by its strings about his neck. "You've got my favorite *learning channel* on there son." he smiled, and added. "Ruby will be in with something for that headache in a minute. Crystal is helping with the new babies."

"Hi Doc! I see you're working late." James said, observing Doc Handles' clothing.

"Yes, I just delivered a baby girl to a couple that were traveling through the area— They're moving to Washington. Then I set a broken finger— two in fact, that got closed in a car door. When I went back to check the new mother, she was delivering the second child that turned out to be a boy. Twins! How about that?" He said with great pleasure.

"WOW! This is the place for twins alright.

"Needless to say, the mother is worn out. They didn't know, they were having twins — traveling and all —. She hasn't checked in with any doctor in a while. Everybody is in good health though. Thank God." Doc added with a tired but happy voice.

"I wonder if those are the emergencies that Crystal was speaking of earlier." Jim inquired absent-mindedly.

"As a matter of fact, yes. We've had only two emergencies tonight. There's not much of, anything that happens around here that the twins don't know about." Doc Handle said with wonder. "They are wonderful people. Once you meet them and they decide to help you. They will always be connected to your life. You will always know them because of what they did to help you. They become part of your thought process. Like —" he hesitated thinking. "they change the way you look at life, your whole attitude," he said with reverence.

"I believe, I know what you're saying. I just got an introduction to *'what they do'*, earlier this evening." Jim said holding up two fingers on each hand and wiggled them all up and down together in the same direction. *(air quote)* "I feel kinda good, energized in a way." He said with wonder.

"I know the feeling. They pulled me out of a *'big funk'* after my wife was killed in an auto accident, a couple years ago." Doc said. "They also, taught me a new way to look at life and death. It has helped me deal with family and friends of patients that either die or are close to death. I look at everything differently now.

"Hey listen! I just thought I would stop by and check on you, before I leave. Someday we'll just sit and talk about things that are sociable, not related to medical problems, but right now I'm beat. I'm going to go home and get as horizontal as it's possible for a body to get. Good night, young man I'll see you tomorrow."

"Good night Doc." Jim said as the older man walked out the door.

Doc met Ruby in the hall. She was headed for Jim's room with his medication. "How did your first encounter go tonight, my dear?" He inquired.

"Pretty good. In fact, he's going to be easy to work with. His thoughts are so open they're right on the surface. We just have to find out what's blocking his memory." Ruby said. "By the way." she added. "When Crystal and I were probing, I sensed a foreign material/drug. It's something, I've not come across before."

"His head injury is more than likely the cause of the memory loss, but I believe this — *whatever* it is may be preventing the recovery of his memory." She added with concern. "I'm anxious the see the results of his blood tests." She lifted the medication tray towards him. "I've got to get this to him." Ruby said turning to leave. "Good night Doc."

"Good night dear," he said, as he turned to head home.

As she entered the room, Jim was pinching the bridge of his nose between both thumbs, his fingers were steepled at his forehead. Clearing her throat quietly, as not to startle him. "Ahem, I've got something for that headache if you're ready." She said quietly.

"Oh please!" He said and lowered his voice to an almost whisper. "I'm ready, this is really *hurting* now." he said, pulling up his sleeve, she noticed sweat beads on his forehead. "If it were possible. I'd say my brain was cross-eyed. You know that feeling?" He mumbled himself into silence.

She swabbed his arm with alcohol and injected the medication, saying nothing. When she finished, she proceeded silently to fluff his pillow, lower the head of his bed, and dim the lights. Ruby placed her hand on his shoulder and pointed at the television with a questioning look on her face, as if to say *"you want the TV on?"*

He shook his head 'no' and immediately placed a hand on his forehead in pain. "Ohh!"

Ruby pulled her shoulders to her ears and whispered silently '*sorry*', as she turned off the television.

Jim whispered back, "It's OK. — My fault." He leaned back and closed his eyes.

Ruby left the room silently after placing a cool damp cloth over his eyes. Her patient slept quietly all night.

When she reached the nurses station, it was empty. While she waited for Crystal to return, she wrote a note to the man with no name. She suggested that he read his notebook sometime during the morning, because he hasn't been able to, with the medication he is taking at night.

# RUN BABY RUN!

As the little man lay in his bed, he reflected on how he had ended up here, in the hospital. "How long have I been in here?" He asked himself more times than he cared to remember. Answering himself, almost disbelieving each time he heard himself say it. "A week... They say five days that's almost a week. It's hard to believe. They said I was unconscious for two days."

His mind was reviewing what had happened. Bits and pieces were coming together but not necessarily in order. Pictures that broke his heart, flashed in his mind. Then the FBI and the police were asking a lot of the same questions. Over and over, again and again. Then he refused to answer any more questions. It made his heart physically hurt to re-live what had happened, over and over, again — they didn't care how he felt talking about it repeatedly. Didn't they hear when I told them the first time? The damn government people must be deaf. They seemed to be more concerned about the missing drugs than whereabouts of his granddaughter.

"Where is my sweet little Sylvia? My granddaughter. They took her. Those animals, took my baby girl." Tears welled in his eyes not for the first time. She was there after school, helping restock the shelves in the in the drug store. She has been coming in every Friday night since she started high school. She had begged him. "Papa! Please, you don't have to pay me very much. I just need a little bit of money for personal things, that mom can't afford to get me. You know like lipstick, make-up or, maybe a necklace or something. Please! Papa please! This way I can buy Birthday and Christmas presents without having to ask for money."

Sylvia had just turned seventeen years old last weekend. She was getting good grades in school. Sometimes she did her homework in the back room of the store. *'cause her mom wasn't home from work yet, and she didn't like being alone.* It wasn't Friday, it was Wednesday. That's what she was doing when those animals robbed the store. Her homework! "Oh God! Don't. Please don't hurt her!" He pleaded as they dragged her out of the back room by her hair. They held a knife to her throat.

They wanted all the money and all the *good* drugs. Which ended up including a shipment of special chemicals. He was holding them for the drug lab in the next town to come and get. They had requested a small amount of the chemicals on short notice so that they can complete a test they're doing. A larger shipment from the big warehouse won't get to them until next week. He had done this before, and thought nothing of it. It was largely an experimental drug, but he only knew of one client that required a few drops in an elixir that was taken by mouth.

These chemicals were stored in his safe normally, but he had just filled the order for the drug-lab and put the containers in a shipping box. They had not been returned to the safe as of yet. Time had slipped by him and he rushed out to lock up, and pull the shades down. It was four minutes past closing time and he must make sure that the customers were all taken care of and ushered out the door. He would lock everything up when the customers, the door locks, and windows were taken care of.

Now he had second thoughts about it. But, all the thinking in the world wouldn't change the fact that they had his granddaughter. "I'll kill them, if I get my hands on them," he said aloud. He cried himself to sleep. And, again he dreamed the whole thing, all over again.

+ + + + +

Jasper Carson, the Pharmacist, was closing up for the night. He was headed to the front of the store to pull the shades down over the windows, and flip the sign over so's it would read "closed" from the street side. When his father and partner in business passed away, he became sole owner. He didn't even have to change the name on the windows. They had "Carson's Pharmacy" neatly printed on them, by a student that needed some extra money. Did a real fancy job of it too.

He noted that there were two young men pushing a grocery basket through the store. They had a few items in the basket disposable razors, shave cream, lots of candy, and other things he can't recall right now. He does remember that they took every item in the basket, with them.

Someone at the front of the store was yelling. He'll never forget. "I think she's having a heart attack. Hey! Mister! Come here and check her."

He trotted to the front of the store to help his elderly cashier, Maggie Penworthy. He found her on the floor, behind the cash register. As he bent down on one knee so he could help her, someone struck him on the back of his head. At first he was confused as to why he was seeing stars. Had he run too fast before bending over? Those questions were going through his mind for the first ten seconds before he realized, *'somebody hit me'*. He fell to the floor from the blow, but blackness didn't completely blind his vision. He hadn't passed out. When his wits returned to him, he was staring into the lifeless eyes of his dear friend, and his cashier, Maggie Penworthy. *Oh! Maggie! I'm so sorry!* He whispered as tears came to his eyes. *"Oh dear."* How was he going to tell her husband, his lifelong friend? Without thinking, he reached up to close her eyes. That was when he saw the blood in her hair. He sucked in a sharp breath noisily. Pushing himself to his feet, turning as he stood. He saw one of the men opening the door to the back of the store. He shouted "Run, Baby run!" He had always called his granddaughter, "Baby."

His tongue became paralyzed when he felt the cold metal on the back of his neck. "Hey Pops! Give me the key to the drug room." The tallest one said as he pressed the gun harder against his spine at the base of his neck.

"Stop that you creep." Sylvia said backing up. She found herself backed into a corner of the small room. She was facing a man who had a nylon stocking pulled over his head, down to his chin. "Get your hands off me. Don't touch me like that." She could see the outline of his penis in the front of his pants. They were stretched tight. He was rubbing his crotch up against her thigh. He was sweating, grunting and licking her neck with his big, fat, ugly tongue. He was like a rutting animal.

She knew that she was in trouble. Just then her grandpa grunted loudly from the front of the store, and it sounded like one of the displays were knocked over. "Hey! We don't have to do this here. If you'll leave my grand-pa alone I'll go with you guys. No fuss. No bother. I promise. Anything you want, just leave him alone. Don't hurt him. Please! He's old. What kind of guys are you anyway? Picking on an old man." She said trying to pull some kind of mercy out of her assailant. "No bargains here missy. You're going with us anyway." The biggest one said.

"You're animals, nothin' but animals." She was screaming and that's when she felt the blow to her head. Damn that hurt. Her vision tunneled into darkness.

From the other room, "I got the key. Let's get this done."

"Bitch" The thug cursed, and dragged Sylvia by her hair, into the store, where he dropped her to the floor. She lay like a rag doll, semi-conscious. She could see her Papa, but couldn't do a thing more than just look at him. He looks alive. She tried to think her thoughts to him. "*Don't move Papa, Please! Don't move. They'll just hit you again. Don't move.*" She blacked out.

"Just don't move." Jasper told himself. For some reason it seemed urgent that he not move a muscle. He felt in danger. He was always the one to say, "Always follow your instincts. They might make you feel foolish, but it's better to be a live fool, than a dead hero." He stayed where he was.

They weren't paying any attention to him, so he was able to watch them through squinted eyes. He slowly, turned his head and was able to see most of what was going on.

They were ransacking the drug supply room. Plundering and spilling everything to the floor that they didn't want. Crushing caplets and pills under their army boots. They took two large boxes of supplies and drugs. Two or three cartons of syringes, the ones he issued to diabetics, for their insulin. There were some with larger needles that were used for measuring, when he was putting special formulas together. Bottles of insulin were also crushed under foot as the animals rummaged the room. Such a big mess created in so short a time.

Sylvia was there on the floor right in front of him. His heart skipped a beat, when his vision cleared enough the see her. He tried desperately to projected his thoughts to her. He had no idea if that was possible to do such a thing but he needed to try anyway. *Baby? Baby are you all right? Dear God please let her be all right.*

When they got ready to leave, they took Sylvia with them. One of the group came over, picked her up, putting her over his shoulder like a sack of grain. "This one's mine." He said as he headed through the door "You can have her when I get through." His laugh brought tears to Jasper's eyes. He couldn't help himself or anyone else for that matter. The pain was almost more than he could bare. A muffled cry escaped him. He tightened his lips, holding any further noise from slipping out, but it was too late. The air he'd been holding, suddenly left him all at once. "Ahhhh!"

The last thing she saw — Looking down at her Papa reaching for her from the floor, *he hadn't followed his instincts, he moved.* and now he curled around a boot that was slamming into his stomach. She screamed "Nooo! Stop!" and again she screamed, "Stop!" as the other boot kicked at his arms, trying to make them let go of the other foot. Her Papa let go when something, *she didn't know what, probably a boot* slammed into his head. His body lay sprawled on the floor, not moving. *Was he still breathing?* She passed out, into darkness again, and hung motionless over the big man's shoulder. He carried her to the pickup truck that waited outside.

+ + + + +

Shortly after he gained consciousness someone was trying to get him to look at some pictures, — Jasper identified three men from pictures that were shown to him. They were three of the of the four guys that escaped from Oregon, State Prison.

"Dear God help her! These men haven't been with a woman in who knows how long." Jasper repeated his silent prayer. "If you're still alive — Run — Baby run."

# THIS OLD HOUSE

The house stood about two hundred yards off the road. Built around 1942, most materials were scrap lumber and unbent nails salvaged from constructions sites around the city. War had taken and taken, there was little if any abundance of anything left. They were still living off of rations like most of the country. This was post wartime and you worked with what you could find. Nobody had money but the big contractors so you scrounged through their 'seconds' or 'throw aways'. Splicing together short pieces of wood, wire or pipe to make them long enough.

You learned to use and re-use, "Back then nothing went to waste or your waist." Grand-ma often told little Scott's mommy. He never forgot what they talked about, what anybody talked about. Especially when they thought he was asleep. He especially remembered them wrestling and laughing in their bedrooms. "You'll understand when you get older son. The grown-ups have their own games.

His Dad was born in this house in 1943. He grew up, served his country, traveled, retired after twenty years with a pension and then settled down at the age of forty-five years old. He married Mommy and she came to live with them. Scott was born three years and seven months later. Mom had miscarried four times trying to give Daddy a child. By then she was forty years old herself. Back then the doctors didn't know of the special problems that befall the child of an older couple.

It wasn't until many years into the future that they studied 'criminal psychology' to any depth. One never knew who the person was they are talking to. Is he normal or just in a state of social acceptance that drugs have created?

+ + + + +

Blackberry vines crawled along the driveway. Shrubs and trees surrounded the house and had grown to tremendous size over the years. There was a small stream that ran through the property. All the plant life thrived and grew into a small oasis. The old house was hidden from the main road.

Scott was the only living relative so it went to him when his grandmother passed on. No one has been here since "Big Scott" went to jail for armed robbery six months ago.

They gave him three years, but he and three other guys broke out the day before yesterday and drove here in a stolen truck which they got rid of. Tonight, when they pulled into the driveway of the old shack, they all jumped out of the truck, raised their hands in the air and gave each other high five's, each slapping the others hand. Laughing with gusto and relief, "We did it. We did it!" They were standing around the truck, "Party time. We got enough stuff to last the rest of the year."

Big Scott grabs the girl and heads for the house, and yells back at the others. "Put the pickup out back, bring the stuff into the kitchen, and put it on the table. Don't touch anything until I can check it out."

Before he dropped her on the bed, he quickly grabbed and whipped the dust-covered bedspread off, on to the floor and dumped the girl on his grandmother's bed. *She is beautiful.* He thought as he rubbed his crotch and shivered, *I haven't touched a woman in eight months. The guys in jail are OK but this is the real thing.* He turned toward the kitchen, thinking to himself. *She's not going to do me any good while she's passed out. I'll wake her up after I straighten out the guys. They're probably pawing through the stuff already. Greedy bastards.*

+ + + + +

Sylvia heard the door close. She lay motionless, in case someone was still in the room. She listened for breathing and heard nothing. She let her eyelids open ever so slightly, and peeked around the room to make sure she was alone. Nobody, thank you Lord Jesus. Her heartbeat sped up, and she breathed a sigh of relief. It was difficult to keep from sneezing with all the dust in the room. She pinched and rubbed her nose and breathed through her mouth. She almost coughed out loud, but she prevented that by pulling the sweater she was wearing up over her nose and mouth. She licked the inside surface of the sweater and then bit down on it, so that the dust would be caught in the moisture instead of coming through the loose knit material. She didn't know why she did that, but it worked. She looked around and found a portrait of an old couple smiling down at her. Probably the guys' grandparents. Looks like the paint is really thin in places. Don't people know you're not supposed to use a cleaner on an oil painting?

*Times wasting.* She told herself, as she went for the window. It was unlocked, but painted shut. *Another door, is it locked?* She tried the handle as quietly as she could, it opens into a bathroom. There was no water in the toilet and the faucets gave no water either. Mmm! She was so thirsty. She'd had nothing to eat or drink since before going to the drugstore. *Papa, please be all right.* The window glass was broken completely out as if someone had broken into the house through here. There was glass on the floor and in the dusty sink. She stuck her head out the window. She could see a road, just through those trees about fifty feet ahead. It was only about six feet to the ground. She reached up, grabbed the top of the window frame, pulled herself up and stuck her feet through the window. Letting go of the window frame she dropped to the ground, on her hands and knees. She stood and leaned against the old building. She inched herself to the corner and peeked around. The men were unloading the truck into the back door of the house. *I have to go the other way* She told herself. Turning she ran to the other corner. *Good, there's some bushes.* Turning again she crept at first, but then ran and leapt into the foliage, only to discover that they were berry bushes. A dozen stupid and unimportant questions flitted through her mind. *What kind? - Blackberry my favor—* "Ouch" She slapped her hand over her mouth, and doing so realized that her sweater was snagged on one-inch thorns. *Brother bear! I asked you not to throw me in the briar patch.* The more she moved, the more snared she got. It was hopeless. She shrugged herself out of the sweater. She had three big scratches on one arm. There was a thorn broken off in her bra. It was poking at her breast, so she tried to pluck it out. *Can't get a hold on it. Later when I've got more time.* She tugged on the sweater material then gave up. It was too tangled to retrieve. She wasn't embarrassed having only a bra on. *It covers more than my bikini top. What am I thinking? Embarrassed?* She whispered, in a daze. *I got'ta get out'ta here. Move Sylvia. Run Baby run!* Memories threatened to overwhelm her. She shook her head to scatter them and prayed. *Oh! Gramps! Please be all right! Dear God help me. Please!* She chided herself. *Move girl! Get out'ta here. Move even if it's wrong. Move now.*

Looking around she saw a ditch, and slipped down towards it. The bottom was muddy and slippery from a recent rain. She lost her footing, and grabbed for some tall weeds that were growing there. They didn't help at all. They pulled right out of the wet soil, roots and all. She landed on her side with a thud, and a squish. "Ohh! Shit" She hissed and again silenced her mouth with her hand. As she pulled her hand away from her face, she saw that it was covered with mud. That gave her an idea. She scooped up some of the mud and smeared it on her arms, legs, face and hair. *Like Rambo.* She told herself. *They can't find me if they can't see me. Damn this isn't going to do my hair any good.* She kept it up until she was covered with mud.

She had to hurry. They would find her missing any minute. She climbed out of the ditch next to but stayed clear of the berry bushes. She bent over and ran parallel to the driveway, while staying behind the bushes. There was a fence at the end of the ditch. She had to squeeze between the fence post and the bushes. The thorns dug deep into her back as she slid past them. This time she didn't make a sound.

She stood, straightened her aching back and winced at the new scratches. She thought she could feel blood dripping or was it a bug crawling on her? It didn't matter. She shouted in her mind *THERE'S A CAR COMING*. It was about a half mile down the road. She didn't want to be seen by her captors, so she ducked into some tall weeds at the edge of the road. "I'll flag'em down when they get closer" She told herself.

As she backed into the weeds, an arm reached out and curled around her waist. She tugged against it and broke free. Stepping toward the road, she started waving her arms at the on-coming car, and she was again caught. This time by the hair, and pulled her to the ground, into the weeds.

+ + + + +

"What was that dear? Did you see — at the side of the road?" As the couple drove past, the husband assured his wife that it was. "*Just some animal ma'dear. Frightened by our car. I'm sure it's just running away.*"

She smiled. "Yes dear. I'm sure you're right. It did look brown all over," she said as they sped away down the road.

Ed and Carol Palmer didn't want to slow down anyway. They had to get their supplies to the store. They owned "Palmer's Catch-all." A little store about twenty miles up the road, in Wide Creek, Oregon. They did a good business. Had just about anything you needed. If they didn't have it, they would 'find it for ya.' That's what they were doing now. Returning home after getting a special order for someone.

+ l + + +

"Ahhh! Ahhh!" said a voice behind Sylvia. "Don't move." It instructed. "You must do everything that you are told. The big man, becomes insane if *anyone* refuses to do his bidding."

"Then why do you stick around? Just leave?" She asked.

"No! I would never do that. This man has my loyalty. He pulled me from deaths' jaws. I will never back stab this man.'

"OK, then talk to me. Make me understand." She pleaded.

"Scott saved my life. He does the evil deeds. He enjoys it." He recounted then continued. "I owe him my life. It is his." He pointed to his heart with a closed fist to his chest. "My job is to see that no one harms him. You must find another way to stop him without harming or killing him. You will not succeed against him as long as I am breathing. You must kill the *evil*, not *him*. I assure you that the *two* are *not* the same. It is not right to kill one, in order to make the other die. I assure you that the man you see is only a shell, a puppet for the evildoer. Do not try to destroy this man. Please! And, I am *warning* you. I *will* stop you.

As he forced her back to the house. "I can't return without you, or he will kill me. My life is his to take, but I will make sure, it is not *you* who makes him take my life."

"Hey! What's going on here? Who goes there?" Yelled one of the guys from the front porch. Wha'cha got there, Rosco?"

"Nothin' that concerns you Grego."

Grego: Short for Gregory, a *sweet* little man, that found out how to survive on the inside. His fellow inmates had hung 'Grego' on him years ago. Nobody messes with Grego except Tuc, now that they're out. Tuc: short for Tucker that's another story, all by itself.

"This belongs to Big Scott." Rosco said and continued speaking under his breath to Sylvia. "Mind my words now, or it's death for you. A very painful death, unlike any other."

"I'm *so honored* that you would tell me these things." She snapped back at him. Speaking very quickly, through her teeth she said. "A painful death vs. a *very* painful death. I know you guys aren't going to let me live. Can't let me live. So, it's up to me, how long I can stand the pain. What do I do then, when I can't stand the pain any longer? Huh? Be a bad girl, so you'll kill me to put me out of my misery?" She said struggling against his hand, full of her hair. Rosco is a foot taller than Sylvia's five foot three inches, so all he has to do is lift upwards. and her feet leave the ground. "I asked you to make me understand. You haven't done that, now have you?" She said accusingly.

Rosco didn't say another word, but lead her, by the hair up the stairs, to the front porch. He stood there, holding her like a trophy, in the doorway.

Scott was coming out of the bedroom, just after discovering that she was no longer there. You could tell he was pissed off, by the look on his face. He had just opened his mouth to shout of her absence, when he spotted her. From anger to disgust in a split second.

When Sylvia saw the sudden change in his face, her heart stood still for the second and third beat. "*Oh my God*" she thought to herself. "*This guy is totally insane. Whacko, Not here! He not only does the evil deed. He is the evil deed.*"

"Take her to the creek out back and bathe that shit off of her." He told Rosco. "Remember." he chided "Don't touch it, Rosco. She's mine first."

"Of course, it shall be no other way. You lead, I follow!" Rosco recited for the ump-teenth time.

"You grovel very well, Rosco." Sylvia snipped at him, as they headed for the small creek about eighty feet behind the house.

"I don't have a death wish. Until I can save his life, I will do whatever it takes to stay alive." Rosco pledged.

"That might take a lifetime Rosco, Look at the guy. He's big, and insane. Who in their right mind is going to go against him?" Sylvia asked.

"Somebody stronger, or crazier than he is." Replied Rosco, "That's the guy I have to look out for, because he'll come after me first to get at him.

"Yeah! Yeah! Lifetime job, Rosco. You're a real loyal guy." She bantered at him. She knew that she shouldn't be chiding him like this. But what did she have to lose? She believed that she was going to die anyway. No way could they let her go now that she could identify them. "So! How many guys have tried to kill him so far? Haven't you paid him back yet?"

Letting go of her hair, and grabbing her hand. Rosco looped a small rope around her wrist. "The creeks down there, don't try anything. Get yourself cleaned up and I'll give you your privacy, or lose it if I have to do it for you," he said, almost fatherly. He continued talking. He couldn't help himself. They made their way to the icy water. He liked her spunk.

"Mostly it's the mud he doesn't like, especially in your hair. His wife always wanted him to spend their summers vacationing in some hot springs mud bath. They went three years in a row. The third year she didn't come back— that's why he was in jail, besides the robbery charges. They were having sex in the mud bath." He informed her.

She interrupted. "EEuuu gross. Isn't that unsanitary? Don't other people have to use the same mud?"

"When he finished." Rosco glared at her for the interruption. "He discovered that her head had slipped under the mud a little too long. Claimed that he thought she was sleeping, like she always did after sex. How was he supposed to know with all that mud everywhere? She always had her eyes closed in bed why not in the mud. Didn't want to get any in her eyes." Rosco said.

"The Jury didn't buy it. I am not his judge. They found him guilty of involuntary manslaughter and robbery when he stole money from other guests that had left the personal items *locked up* (they thought) in the shower and changing rooms."

She finished as best she could, considering the ice-cold water, no soap, and that damn rope tied to her. *Damn thing got tighter and stiffer with cold water on it. It was making her hand numb.* He tugged her back to the house with the rope. As they entered the house through the kitchen door, Scott grabbed the rope and dragged her to the bedroom. On the way he snatched a couple beers, two ready-made sandwiches, and then flung her on the bed with the food and beer. He cut the rope off of her when he saw that her fingers were turning blue, like she was complaining about.

Thinking to herself. *'Good! Those filthy blankets are gone.'* My Allergies —.

Still holding the knife, Scott sat on the bed with his legs crossed, leaning on the shelves that formed a headboard above the head of the bed. He opened one of the sandwiches and began eating. After washing down part of his sandwich with a beer. "I brought those in for you," he told her, pointing at the other beer and sandwich with the knife. That's all you're getting, so eat it *now.*"

Thinking at about fifteen words per second. *Try to stall this guy. Don't piss him off. Please! I don't wanna feel any pain. OH! God please!!! Help me!* She picked up the sandwich and fussed with the plastic seal of the package. Her fingers were cold and numb from the icy water. Her body was shaking, all she had on was her bra, jeans and tennis shoes, which were all soaking wet and cold.

The knife flicked in front of her and was gone before she could react. He had pierced the plastic of her sandwich wrapper. She thought to herself. *So much for stalling.* She cleared her dry nervous throat as she peeled the plastic wrapper off the sandwich. Before she could take a bite—.

"Grab hold of that beer." Scott instructed.

She did as she was told.

"Hold it sturdy against your knee." He said as he used the tip of the knife to pop the top open.

"You're pretty good with that thing." She smiled nervously.

"Don't make me show you *how good*, Sweetheart." He boasted. "Just do *what* you're told without argument, and we'll get along just fine. What's your name?"

"Sylvia," she offered. "What's yours?"

"Scott," he offered, "Last name too, come on," he probed, rotating the knife over and over in one hand.

"Tempest, Sylvia Tempest." She said. "What's *your* full name?"

"Scott. 'Big Scott' that's all you need to know.

She took a deep breath and said. "Let me add right now, that if you're planning on having sex with me try to remember, that I am new at the sex thing. Please don't get mad if I don't do it right."

"HA! HA! HA!" He burst out, surprising himself. "Nice try little girl. They teach you that in self-defense class? Get the guy to feel sorry for you? Did they ever tell you that once a *real man* gets hold of you, it ruins you for anybody else? You won't want anybody else, because he was so good. Nothing else is ever as good. He leaves you wanting him even if you know that he'll hurt you again." He said nodding short, slow strokes with his head, then lowered his chin and raised his eyebrows. He leaned directly at her face.

She sat cross-legged, diagonally across the bed from him. She was leaning against a bedpost at the foot of the bed, trying to get as much distance between them as possible. Then instantly things changed. In the time it took him to lean across the bed, his face had changed totally. She knew that she had met the *other one*. The *evildoer*. She knew in an instant that there would be no resistance given to *this one*. She could not, would not banter with *this one*. What was she to do? Bantering had always been her defense when she was in a situation she felt uncomfortable in, Acting tough was her most powerful defense around the school bullies. It was very obvious that this situation called for something else. This was not the man that fed her the sandwich and beer just moments ago.

He was on her in an instant. He had grabbed her crossed ankles and pulled her across the bed to the middle. One hand was holding both ankles and the other was reaching up under/between her legs.

*Dear God! Help me! My body is betraying me!* She screamed inside her head. "Mmmm — this is not supposed to feel — good, but —." She tried to resist. "Mmmm." She groaned involuntarily. She found her pelvic area lifting itself pushing against his hand. She groaned as her hips picked up a sensual rhythm and volunteered themselves to gyration. She climaxed. She was beside herself with shame, embarrassment and fear all wrapped up in this wonderful, lusty feelings that still moved through her. She was breathing hard, gasping for air. He was lying next to her now, he locked her eyes with his. This was too much— she passed out. The moment he spoke, she awoke but pretended to be knocked out.

"Hey!" he was amazed. "Damn I must be pretty good." He waited a full minute and then he shook her. "It's not break time, you're still dressed. Now get those pants off. We're not through yet." He ordered, put the tip of the knife blade under each bra straps and severed them one at a time. Lastly cutting the bra away, between her breasts with a flick of his wrist.

"I need to get off the bed so I can pull my jeans off." She counseled.

Letting go of her ankles he motions her off the bed with the knife. He also stood up and removed his clothes.

After peeling her cold wet shoes, jeans and panties, she stood there shivering. Big Scott was larger than any she had ever seen before.

"Now look at yourself in the mirror. I know you've looked at yourself in the mirror before. Touched yourself before. Haven't you? Don't lie — I'll know." He prodded.

"It's natural for a human to explore himself," she said honestly.

"OK." He said patiently. He became aroused as she followed his orders to pose in different positions for his inspection.

She did what she was told. She watched herself in the mirror as he touched her here and there. Her legs stiffened and she almost fell off the chair he had told her to set in. She saw him, taking care of himself and thought. *Oh good. Maybe he'll leave me alone. I don't want him angry with me. He hasn't had sex with me yet.* She hears herself saying. "Now. What can I do for you?" *Oh! Dear God. I'm sorry! I'm soo mixed up. I just don't want him angry with me. I'm sorry! I'm afraid of the pain he could make me feel.*

"Nothing," he said walking to the door and unlocked it. Stuck his head out and told Rosco. "Get Tuc in here."

*Oh! God no!! No! No!!* Tears immediately sprang to her eyes.

He held the door until Tuc knocked to get in. When he knocked, Scott spoke into his ear.

Watching the two men talk quietly gave her the creeps. Her situation had changed. Tuc, the man speaking to Scott was taller than Scott's' five-foot eleven inch by about five or more inches. *He's a giant. He must weight three hundred pounds. Not an ounce of fat on those iron pumping, ebony muscles.* He was looking at her over Scott's shoulder and nodding his head slowly, listening to Scott's instructions.

"Bring us all some cold beers on your way back." He said, as Tuc turned to leave the room. Scott said, "When Tuc gets back in here, we're going to have a cool beer and get to know each other better." He instructed. "Tucker, don't call him that to his face. Tuc has a really *deep* desire to be *with* you. You *are* going to let him do *whatever* he wants. Do you understand?" he said almost friendly.

"Yes Sir." *Please don't let him hurt me. Please!* She said tugging on the sheet, to cover herself. It wouldn't budge with him sitting on it.

He looked down and smiled at her efforts. "Ah! Ah! Ah! We'll have none of that either little lady. Get up here on the bed and we'll get you ready for him." He patted the bed.

Reluctantly, she climbed on the bed, and sat knees together on the corner.

He reached over grabbed her arm, spun her around as if she were a featherweight. He grabbed her leg and dragged her across the bed next to him, where he sat leaning against the headboard.

She didn't know what he had in mind until she did as she was told. As she seated herself his hand massaged her again. "Mmm" She whispered a groan.

"Look at my face. Look in my eyes," she turned her face as instructed. His other hand was busy taking care of himself while he watched the change come across her face and into her eyes.

Ahhh! Mmmm! She moaned with the shock of new feelings.

"Get on your hands and knees," he ordered impatiently.

As he continued, she found herself pushing back against him.

"Mmm look at the greed this little girl/woman has." He suddenly jumped out of bed and squirted semen all over his grandparents' picture, then flung the portrait to the floor, and shouted. "Are you happy now?" He spat at them. "Was that good enough for you, this time?"

# LITTLE SCOTT

Scott's parents were out of town on a second honeymoon. They were going to return in two weeks. He had been sleeping over at his grandparents' house, every summer he could remember. *This* summer, on his first night there, it was a very hot and humid night and he slipped into bed under a single sheet, with nothing on. He missed his friend, Sammy. They used to masturbate together. See who could shoot the farthest. Sometimes they would touch each other. Boy he could really shoot a long way when Sammy did him.

All he had to do was *think* of Sammy, and he'd get hard. He had learned to bring toilet paper with him (to shoot in) when going to bed. As he laid there this first night, the bed was shaking with his excitement. When finished, his body settled and he dropped the tissue in the basket beside the bed.

"That was lovely dear. You did that very nicely."

He stopped in mid-breath. He would have bolted from the bed if he'd had any clothes on but he didn't. So, he sat there frozen, dumbfounded and speechless. Slowly at first, then quickly he began sucking in much needed air into his lungs.

"Did it feel, as good as it looked sweetheart?" He had not heard his grandparents enter the room. There they were. Grand-pa and grand-ma were leaning back on a small couch in the corner of this spare room he was to sleep in for the next two weeks. They were right there.

"Please don't be upset. *Everybody* touches themselves. I hope you don't think you're the only person to discover that it feels good. We were wondering when you would start exploring yourself. We aren't here to embarrass you, but to make sure that you do it properly and get the most pleasure out of it that you can."

And they did, every morning and every night during those two weeks he was there.

They wouldn't let up on him. They taught him about creams and lotions. When he had difficulty, all he had to do was close his eyes and visualize Sammy. He never told them about Sammy.

He was twelve that first time. His parents would never have believed him if he told on his grandparents. He would be too embarrassed 'cause he'd be telling on himself. The nights of each summer were mixed with a torrent of emotions. They would all retire early. The boy was supposed to pretend like his grandparents weren't in the dark corner. He was to touch himself while striking poses that would show them his pleasures. He was to prolong it as long as possible. This continued every summer until he went away to college, where Sammy and he shared a small apartment.

Sammy found another love, a girl that first year away. He tells Scott "You should try it. Girls feel good."

So, Scott did. He married the first girl he dated. They'd had no children. They were not married but four years when the tragic "*accident*" happened. Now here he was. Running away from the law.

# SYLVIA

Scott was standing by the dresser, when Tuc came back in the room and sets the beers on the nightstand. Pulling his clothes off as he climbed onto the bed, he laid on his back and told her to sit on him.

He was huge. She couldn't... it hurt too much.

"That's OK little one, just prop yourself up on your knees. Say are you thirsty? I think one of those beers is already open. Why don't you drink it before it gets flat and warm? That's right just reach over there and get it."

Silvia's throat was so dry. She didn't drink but a few sips of the beer that Scott had given her earlier. She didn't like the taste. She'd had nothing to drink since before she went to the drugstore after school. She drank half the can before stopping. "Sorry! You want some?" She offered.

"No thanks! I'm not thirsty right now. Why don't you move around on me a little?" He said calmly.

After about five minutes. She wanted him. It didn't hurt as much this time. Soon she couldn't stop herself. "Mmm, Mmm, you're not through, yet are you?" Sylvia asked.

"That's OK baby, Grego has a nice big one for you. He motioned to the little man who had been watching from the side of the bed. Come on over here Grego." Tuc said satisfied.

She was off of the bed and pulling at Grego's clothes. Tugging and pulling until he was naked. She pushed him onto the bed and began to kiss him everywhere. He didn't take her. Her kisses were enough to bring him the satisfaction he needed. With that and all the drinking he'd been doing he slept afterwards.

Her bare back side, was more than Scott could stand. He climbed up onto the bed and took her from behind. *Sammy! Oh Sammy!* Holding onto her hair, pulling her head back as he took her.

Thinking to himself, "Damn I must be good, that's the second time she's passed out. She must have had enough. She's not begging for anymore. She's probably exhausted." He reached down on the floor and retrieved the rope, tied her ankle to the bedpost. He passed out with the group on the bed.

# MORNING AFTER

Curiosity, got the best of Rosco. He had been up for almost an hour. He cracked the bedroom door open after he'd heard nothing but snoring. "You guys going to sleep all da— damn! The smell hit him right away. Rosco grabbed the front of his shirt and pulled it up over his mouth and walked to the bed where they all lay in a heap of tangled arms and legs. On close examination he saw white foam coming out of the girl's mouth. Somebody had used the bed for a toilet. Her head dangled at an odd angle, and she had messed herself. *One of these damn fools had broken her neck.* He untied her ankle and laid her on the bedspread that was on the floor, dust rose into the air making golden shafts of the light coming through the windows.

He shook Scott's shoulder. "Come on man we got a problem. The girl is dead."

Scott stirred and then his eyes popped open. "What the fu——? What? Who shit on me?" He roared.

The other two woke up immediately. Wide-eyed trying to get their brains to accept what they saw.

The girls' bladder and bowels were released when she died. The smell was bad. Grego ran to the bathroom and vomited in the dry toilet.

They all walked down to the creek and cleaned up as best as they could. Got dressed and went to the kitchen. It was about seven thirty in the morning. They had to make plans. The only concern for the girl was — *how to get rid of the body.*

"The House is hidden from the road. Water and gas need to be turned on. No electricity though 'cause the lights can be seen from the road. We've got candles. Keep those flashlights pointed at the ground. We don't need anyone dropping by to say 'howdy' or sell us a vacuum.

"Rosco would you please?" Scott asked "See if you can turn some of those groceries, we got last night into something edible? There's probably some pots and pans in the cupboard. See if there's a pot for hot water. We've got lots of instant coffee. There are more than likely some cups too.

Rosco replied without delay. "Sorry boss, but I never learned much about cooking'. I could boil water for the instant coffee.

"I can cook a little bit." Grego jumped in, anxious to get out of the room and away from the horror.

"OK." Scott said "See what you can do with what we got."

+ + + + +

Grego had whipped up a pretty good omelet. It was more or less scrambled eggs mixed with diced beef jerky, tomatoes, and cheese. Flour tortillas heated over the stove burner. Everybody said it wasn't bad at all. There was a big pot of hot water on the stove. All you had to do was dip out a cup hot water and stir in some instant coffee. *Serve your own coffee.* That didn't work out, so Grego poured instant coffee in the pot of water.

"We're going to have to do something else about lunch and dinner." Grego worried. "Eggs is just about all I ever learned how to cook."

After breakfast, they all sat around talking about the good sex they had last night. The little girl was really turned on too.

Tuc said that he had put something in the beer, like Scott had asked him to.

"What *was* the stuff you put in it?" Scott asked.

"I don't know. The box said 'experimental laboratories'. It was in one of those cardboard mailing boxes we took from the drugstore." Tuc replied.

"Well, whatever it was it made her want more, and more." Grego contributed. "Like 'Spanish fly', it made her hot. She couldn't get enough."

"I was hoping it might make her pass out, so we could all get what we wanted, without too much fuss. After all there was only one of her, and four of us. She went crazy." Tuc informed everybody, and asked. "What are we going to do with her now?"

# CLUES

Kathy brought in Jim's breakfast tray with a note from the twins. "Good morning! I hope you're hungry." She said with a bright smile. "I see you've already showered. I'll change your bed after we finish serving breakfast." She put the tray on the lap table. Adjusting the height of the table, she rolled it over to where he sat in a chair. "I'll see you in a little while. Breakfast smells good, best eat, while it's hot," she said leaving the room to serve the other patients.

"Humm? What's this? A note— let's see what it says," he said aloud to no one in particular. He was by himself, but read the note aloud, as if he would understand it better, if he heard it out loud.

*Good morning!*

*We hope that you rested well last night. We have a job for you this morning. Your chart shows that you have had pain medication in order to ease your headache at night. This takes away your opportunity to review your note-book before going to sleep. It is important for you to do this. Please review your book this morning. It is very important that you spend your time relaxing until we get there. We will be using a lot of energy today.*

*See you at 10 a.m.*

*Ruby & Crystal*

He told himself aloud, after reading the note. "Hmm a lot of energy? Well, the *relax* part I'm gettin' *really* good at. I'll take a nap after I eat

"Good morning Carl!" It was Captain Kennar.

"Carl?" Jim smiled. "Carl for sure? — Damn that's great!"

"Don't get too excited," he winked at Carl and placed his first finger in front of his lips. "The FBI is planted just outside your door here. They showed up at my office, at the same time these reports hit my desk. They wanted to take you into custody but Doc Handle said that it would interfere with your recovery to remove you from the hospital at this time. Said that you were going through some therapy, with a couple of his technicians." The Captain informed him.

"Finish your breakfast while it's hot son. I'll fill you in on what I've learned so far while you eat." he said while pulling a chair closer to Carl's bed.

"OK Captain, let me hear what you've got." Carl said hungrily consuming his meal. "Oh! By the way I have a *therapy* session this morning, the *technicians* will be here at ten." He said handing the note to Wayne.

Wayne nodded. "That's good news. Now here's some more. Your full name is Carlton Frederick Bridgeman. You're thirty-one years old. Long light auburn hair, green eyes. You don't need corrective lenses, and you're willing to donate all useable organs and glands. You're still covered on your life/health policy. So, your stay here is paid for. Your coverage will last until your memory comes back and, or your therapy is completed. That's a good policy."

"That takes a big load off of my mind. Maybe some of the stress I'm feeling will ease off now that I know I'm not in debt up to my eyeballs for all this help I'm getting."

"You have eight thousand five hundred dollars cash coming as soon as you claim it. That's from your bike insurance. It covers repairs and personal loss. Didn't think you'd mind if I inquired about your insurance

"Not really, it's helpful information. Personal loss? Ha!" He hooted. You mean they're going to pay me so I can buy a new memory? What happens when I find my old one? Do I pay the money back? I'm sorry." Carl quipped. "I'm only kidding. I'm feeling a little *pulled apart* right now. Hey! How do you know all this about me? I don't even know *that* much myself!"

"Pure genius young man. Pure genius!" Wayne said as he handed Carl a wallet that was made of leather. Before he let go of the wallet, just as Carl was touching it Wayne felt a tingling sensation and an almost a mental spark, when he let go of it.

Carl didn't know that Wayne had felt anything but when he touched his wallet he said. "Damn! This *is mine*! I can tell you right now. This is *my* wallet. He whispered almost inaudibly but with excitement. "I can't tell you by looking at it, but it *feels* like *mine*," he said closing he eyes fingering the well-worn leather.

"Keep it down son. If the government gets curious it could take three months to open that wallet. They don't know about it yet." Wayne said as he stepped between Carl and the open door to the room. Would you like me to lock it up for you? I could pass it to your 'technicians' on my way out. He offered.

"Here take this." Carl said handing the wallet back to Wayne after he slipped the paper money out of it. "I don't know *what's* in my past, but I *do* want to be the *first* to find out. Those guys look like they'd eat me for lunch. One of them even has a toothpick in his mouth. Look at that." Carl said while inconspicuously pointing with his nose, towards the door. "This should keep me in sodas until I can get some insurance money."

Wayne didn't have to ask how much money there was 'cause he put the cash in the empty wallet. There's just something about Carl. Wayne didn't know why, but he knew the kid was innocent of wrong doing in this case. It seemed so obvious to him. He didn't like the FBI bugging the kid either.

"How did you get hold of my wallet?" Carl inquired.

"Bartender turned it into the police, when you didn't return to get it. Told the cops you left with some guys in military clothing. They ran your name through the DMV files. Got your print off the back of the drivers' license. Prints got tagged as a match for the ones you gave us. And voila! Here it is."

Wow! This is great." Carl smiled showing a lot of teeth. "So cool!"

"Genius! I tell you." Wayne said proudly, then put his foot on the chair, leaned over to tie his shoe and spoke in a whisper. "FBI don't know about it. You're going to need it for your ten o'clock meeting." He smiled sneakily. "FBI's going to make a big deal out of this, if they find out.

Have one of the girls secure it in the safe when you're through." Then he stood up and said signaling with his eyes to the restroom. "Open it only during your very private times. I think, it might be important to your treatment, to be with the twins the first time

"Those guys outside." Wayne said. "I'm not leaving them alone out there. I've got a twenty-four hour post out there too. Something tells me they're not above sneaking around to get what they want. And, never ever tell them they can't do something. They'll have the rule they follow, *changed* by yesterday. From the way I understand it, they're waiting around *just in case* you're involved in the drugstore robbery / kidnapping. They don't want you going anywhere. We'll talk more about that later. Not to worry son not to worry." He patted Carl's shoulder reassuringly.

Carl sighed "Thanks Wayne. I am speechless at your generosity. Your kindness has eased my misgivings about this situation. The twins are something else too!"

The intercom leapt to life. *"Captain Wayne Kennar please call the operator. Captain Wayne Kennar please call the operator."* Wayne said. "Excuse me!" and reached for the phone on Carl's nightstand. He pressed '0' and got the operator. "This is Captain Kennar, answering your page— Yes, — "Would you ring me through please? — Thank you." He said and was connected directly to Headquarters. "This is dad Jill, what's up? — OK, I have one stop to make on the way in, but I'll be there shortly. Thanks baby!" He hung up the phone. "I think my daughter is as anxious the help out on the case as I am. Her name is Jill. She works at the department. Has for three years now." Wayne said proudly as his smile widened then turned to a frown.

"She was injured in the same accident that took my wife— her mother." He said and swallowed hard and stood in one spot for a few seconds. "She's in a wheel chair now, but that doesn't slow her down." He bowed his head full of memories.

Carl cocked his head slightly. "What does she do there?"

"She's a switchboard operator." He raised his head smiling proudly. "And a radio dispatcher. She took the emergency call from Danny Coachman right after he saw you flyin' out of that van. She's been hooked on this case ever since." Wayne said proudly. "I believe she thought Danny was kidding at first, 'cause she asked him. 'Who would throw somebody else away?' God bless her! She's independent as can be. Has her own apartment, even." He boasted. "The twins have been a 'God send'. They lifted her right up spiritually. She thought the accident was her fault some how. She thought her punishment was *being saved.* That way she *had to watch* the pain, and grief that her mothers' death had caused. They showed her the truth about life and death. She's A-OK now. Thank God—." He paused a moment. "Hey! Listen I got'ta run, got some more answers waitin' at the station.

"Thanks again, Wayne! Let me know if you find *anything else.* Please!" Carl pleaded.

"Not to worry son. You'll be first— right after me." Wayne assured him. "You through with lunch?"

Carl sat staring at nothing anyone could see. He replied absent-mindedly "Mmm! Yes, food is my last thought now."

"I can understand that. Here let me take this tray out for you," Wayne offered. "You need to get some rest, before ten o'clock gets here. The twins are very prompt." With the wallet in hand, Wayne picked up the tray keeping the wallet underneath and left the room, walking right by the two federal agents. He nodded and spoke to his man as he left. "Good night Thomas."

"G'night Sir." Thomas nodded.

Wayne said under his breath. "Stay sharp son. I don't trust these guys. Get one of the nurses to be with him if you need a break," he warned. "Anything happens, *call me* ASAP at the station. They can find me. These guys have no reason to be inside of this room. Remember that 'no reason' at all."

"Yes sir. I understand. Captain!??" The officer said, to be assured that he had his boss's full attention. Because what he said next was barely audible. "Sir, my replacement will need to be informed before arriving, because I can't hand down orders verbally while the other agents are present. I don't want the leave the area in order to transfer the information. Sir."

"Very good young man. I'm impressed." Wayne smiled broadly at the rookie. "Pretty soon you can be an FBI agent too!" Wayne said and lightly tapped the young man's arm. He had a good rapport with his men. He winked at the kid.

"Thank you but please sir, I don't wan'ta end up like those guys. Nobody likes you 'cause they're scared of ya." Thomas screwed his face up with mock distaste. "Good night, sir." He added with a smile that disappeared, as he returned to duty.

# JOURNEY

"Carl! Carl!? He didn't recognize his name, so Ruby placed her hand on his arm. He stirred slightly, turned on his side, and mumbled. "He's in a dream state." She told Doc Handle who was standing next to Crystal on the other side of the bed. Doc loosely wrapped a blood pressure cuff around Carl's arm but did not tighten it. He just wanted to be able to check the blood pressure quickly if he had to.

Doc also had three different medications ready if needed. He had received the blood test results. There was a large amount of a rarely used chemical plus two others in his system. Mostly it is used in psychiatric units with uncontrollable patients. It lets the body function but not the brain's fear center. It all but completely shuts down the psychotic mind. A person on this medication can appear and act somewhat normal. Without it they would be a danger to themselves and everyone around them. In rare circumstances it would, if ever be approved for pharmacy distribution. Right now, it's restricted to institutional facilities where the patient is under constant supervision. There have been no studies of the effect it would have on a person with normal behavior patterns."

"This drug takes a long time to leave the body when small doses are used" Doc informed everybody. "Carl had a large amount of the stuff in his blood. Lord only knows how long it will take to leave his body. Was there going to be permanent damage? What could possess someone, to inject a drug that they didn't know what it was into another person?" He shook his head; he just couldn't understand. "I know evil when I see it and I can tell it's been in contact with this situation."

Crystal asked Doc in a soft voice. "Lloyd? Are you OK? Something wrong?"

The twins were aware of the chemicals in Carl's' body, and what the dangers to Carl were. Doc whispered. "Yeah! I'm OK. I'm just pondering the cruelty of mankind. Sometimes it really gets to me. It's just that this anger that comes over me when I think about it sometimes. Some people are not human.

"Mmm. Hey Doc!" Carl said stretching, yawning and then stopping when he noticed that his room was full. "Oh! Hi everybody! You guys look different in your street clothes. I like this better, not that your hospital gear is bad." He smiled.

"These *are* more comfortable." Crystal volunteered.

Ruby cleared her throat to get everyone's attention, "Ahem! I think we should get started, while he's still relaxed. Is everybody ready?"

They all nodded, including Carl.

Ruby started by saying, "Carl, I want you to close your eyes and take a deep breath and let it go as slowly as you can." She paused and watched him follow her instructions. "That's right. Let it out until you believe there's not even a little bit of air in your lungs. That's good

Carl was feeling more relaxed, the more she spoke.

"Now very slowly, inhale through your nose until you have every inch of your lungs so full of air they couldn't hold more if you tried. That's right sit up, let your chest stick out, make more room for the good healthy air to soak into your lungs. Now slowly, with your mouth and throat open wide. Exhale, just letting the air come out of you without pushing until you're completely empty. Exhale slowly, that's right. Now close your eyes. Not tight. Relax. That's good. I want you to do this again, about three or four more times. I'm going to lower the head of the bed, while you do this. If you start feeling light-headed, just speed up the exercise a little. You're probably breathing too slowly."

Carl smiled. He felt good, as he continued the slow breathing. He felt as if he were almost floating. Ruby's soothing voice drifted in the background.

From this point forward there was *not one word* spoken in the room. Ruby's and Crystal's special twin talents took over. They were in Carl's mind communicating with him.

Ruby instructed Carl further, as to what was to happen during this procedure. "You may feel someone touch your shoulder, arm, or other parts of your body, and this will not distract you. You will hear only the voices of Crystal and myself. You are safe here."

"The doctor is here to assure that you are physically out of harm's way. You might feel the blood pressure cuff tighten on your arm. That doesn't mean there is any kind of problem. He is here to monitor you physically nothing more. Nothing can harm you here."

"You will *see without feeling* where any pain is coming from and tell us about it. The actions and the pain that you see have already happened in your past, and cannot harm you now. We are going to bring back some facts that were lost to you in your recent past. There is a chemical in your body that you will be able to detect. It is blocking your memory. You will be able to find another path around this, to your lost memories. Once you find this path, you will never lose it. It is a strong path. Once the drug has lost its ability to block your memory, it will dissipate. Your body will force it out of your system naturally. If you understand, please nod your head."

Carl, nodded.

Now he heard Crystal's voice. "Hello Carl. There is something that I want to tell you. Nod your head, if you hear my voice."

Carl nodded.

"Good." Crystal said without moving her lips. Everything that she said to him was inside Carl's head. "Now instead of nodding your head I want you to say the word 'yes' in your head. We will hear you just like you are hearing us right now. Our lips are not moving. Open your eyes and look at me now as I speak to you."

Carl opened his eyes and saw that she was truly speaking without moving her mouth. He tried to think something to her, but couldn't. His mind had too many thoughts trying to get out.

Ruby's voice floated in and he looked at her as she communicated to him. "Carl you're breathing to fast, that uses up energy. Please go back to your breathing exercises. He closed his eyes, disappointed. That's right. Slowly. Deep. Slow. Don't make any breathing sounds. Expand the muscles around your lungs, don't make the air push the muscles out. Good. Slow. Close your eyes. That's better. We are going to the basement to find your lost memories. Picture yourself stepping onto an escalator that *you* control the speed of. Your first steps are going to be slow. You control the speed. All you have to do is squeeze this switch handle." She said as she placed a *soft 'Nerf ball'* in his hand. "This is a *pressure* sensitive switch, you need only to *softly* squeeze the handle to make it work." She told him this because she didn't want him using his physical energy on a mental tool. "When you step onto the escalator tell us the first memory that comes to you. Look down the steps of where your memory is. Remember we're sharing. Show us what comes to you first?"

Crystal and Ruby waited with Carl. "All your memory is stored down there. Just relax and you will move toward your strongest memory. Do it."

"Only you can bring your thoughts out for inspection. You need to bring it to the surface so that we can see it *with* you. We cannot see it without you. Your private thoughts are safe unless you bring them to the surface. Now let's walk toward the escalator."

"Yes! I understand." He thought to them, and grinned.

Ruby told them both that they needed a break. This is very tiring for the twins.

Ruby told Carl that the *next time* they got together they would use less energy because he already had the instructions needed. He knew what to do. She would hand him a note in *her handwriting only* with the word *Escalator* hand written on it. (This was so that the trance couldn't be accidentally triggered if he saw it written somewhere else.) She showed him her hand writing in his head. He would immediately come back to this place that they are in now. And, be in the same state of mind and relaxation. "We are going to *pull back* now and everything will be as it was before we came here." Ruby informed.

As they all came back to here and now. They remained silent, thinking to themselves. Dr. Lloyd Handle tightened the pressure cuff on Carl's arm and after a minute said, "All seemed normal here."

"Today is our usual day off. It's not even ten thirty. We have a couple of things to do this morning." Crystal said tiredly, "Tell you what. Let's get together after lunch today." She paused. "Say about one o'clock"? She looked around for approval.

Doc said that he didn't believe he had to be there for the next session unless they were uncomfortable without him.

Ruby said that it would be OK. They could call him in if they needed. They were all going to be somewhere in the hospital anyway.

Doc finished taking Carl's pulse and told him, "Before the meeting this afternoon it would be beneficial if you read through your notebook and add anything new that you have thought of."

"OK Doc! That sounds like a good idea," he said as he watched him leave the room. Getting out of bed he walked to the door of his room before he remembered the guards. He asked Thomas if he would get him a Pepsi from the machine. Thomas declined but offered to escort him to the soda machine. "After all you're not a prisoner here." he said loud enough for the FBI guys to hear.

Thomas locked the room, before they walked down the hall.

It only took one FBI agent to follow them.

They were walking down the hall and a guy with two fingers bandaged walked by, nodded 'hello' and went on about his way to the door. Thomas and Carl watched the little man leave the building and get into a beautiful little turquoise on white 1953 Chevy pickup truck. It looked to be very well cared for and they both agreed that it was a nice looking truck. Carl spent an extra twenty seconds looking at the truck through the window, before he turned the corner to the soda machines. He didn't know what it was but there was something about the truck that seemed to trigger a feeling he didn't recognize. It made him feel uncomfortable and he wasn't sure why. He let it pass because he'd had so many strange feelings lately. *It was probably nothing.*

When they got back to Carl's room Thomas reached out and unlocked the door. Carl smiled and tipped his head in recognition to the FBI agents as they both entered his room and Thomas closed the door behind them.

'Excuse me." Thomas said. "Mind if I stay a minute? Just long enough the let those guys know that they don't have control? I know they're dying to find out what we're doing and saying in here with the door shut

"Stay as long as you like. I really don't mind." Carl said smiling.

"A couple of minutes will do, just as a reminder." Thomas said mischievously, as he walked to the window. "The guys in the pickup truck look like they're arguing. They haven't left yet."

Carl turned to see the truck right outside *his* window. It was a little odd to watch someone that couldn't see you. They watched as the argument calmed down and the pickup drove away. The hairs on the back of Carl's neck stood at attention. He felt goose flesh rise on his arms. Carl shrugged it off for the fact that he was eavesdropping on a private argument. None of his business. He turned away from the window, toward the bed and got in feeling tired.

Thomas asked. "Is there was anything I could do before I return to the hall?"

Carl was using the controls to lower the head of the bed, leaned back and closed his eyes. "No. Thanks anyway. I think I'll take a nap until lunch."

"Rest easy now. I'm right outside if there's a problem." Thomas said as he closed the door behind him.

When Carl was alone, he pulled out the notebook from under the mattress. He held the book between both hands and closed his eyes. He could think of nothing else that was new to add to the pages but decided to review them anyway.,

*So far, he had:*
Motorcycle - Honda 500 -On beach/over cliff.
Had a dirt bike sold it - $ for the trip I'm on. Where from?
Feeling too late if I don't hurry.

Tattoo - upper left arm - single rose - "Rose" is a name.
Hot springs - waterfall - Colorado River? Arizona?
Heel on edge, almost fell over. Very frightened. - Last memory before park, George and Sara.
Where is that cliff????
White van - not a memory - was told.
Feeling — Why would someone throw me away like trash?
Playing pool — location unknown — looking down the end of a pool stick.

I see money laying on the side of the pool table. - I see the girl leaning back, with her head on the wall in corner. Big sunglasses — can tell that she's young. "She doesn't look well— probably drunk, arm hanging down - legs spread apart, not very lady like of her, probably passed out. She isn't your problem—

After Carl read the list, he sat silently willing himself to remember forgotten things, places and people. He fell into a fitful nap.

There was nothing that seemed to be clear. There was a wall that looked to be made out of Multi-colored, pastel crystals with a smooth, flat, scale like surface very much like mica. This wall has very large, flat wafer or scale like sheets. One on top of the next forming the wall.

*Mica is related to aluminum silicate minerals, characteristically splitting into flexible sheets used in insulation and electrical equipment. Often used in furnace windows.*

He was plucking at one of the largest crystals when it came away in his hand with little effort, he couldn't see through the wall because of its' thickness and the curve of the passageway or tunnel like hole. "Yes!" He told himself. "When I saw it from up on the hill, I could see that there is another side to this a wall. — Another way out," he said. Then asked "Out of where? Out of the wall or out of where I was before he found the wall." It was giving him a headache.

Without making up his mind to do so he was drawn *inside of* the tunnel. *Inside* of the wall. He crawled deeper into the tunnel, before long it curved upward to the left and then curved again to another angle and direction, then it narrowed. He was within inches of the walls other side and its outside layer, his way out. He stretched his arms out but could not come in contact with the other side. He was stopped by the shrinking size of the tunnel ahead of him, and a layer of crystals like the one he had just pulled from the other side of this wall to get in here. He needed to go back to get some tools so he could enlarge this area and knock the crystalline scales off of the other side. He needed help.

His arms were stretched over his head as he tried to reach the other side of the wall. He pushed himself with his legs into the narrowing tunnel. He had wedged himself in tight. He was stuck. There was no hand or foothold for him to push or pull against. *Dear God! What to do now.* It felt as if the wall had wrapped itself around him. He had the picture in his mind of being trapped inside of one of those 'Japanese finger traps'. A toy he used to have as a kid. You put a finger inside of each end of this tube that was made out of woven basket grass. The harder you tried to pull your fingers apart the tighter it got. There was no escape until you relaxed your fingers and pushed instead of pulling.

He was near panic when he felt a hand on his right ankle and someone was pulling him out of the tunnel backwards and very quickly. His eyes flew open and looked upon the pretty face of Sara. She was in uniform. The nurse had let her in. Her look of concern turned into a smile as he opened his eyes. She let go of his ankle and placed her hand on the bed railing.

"Hey pretty girl. Nice to see ya!" Carl smiled back sleepily and sighed with the relief of being out of the trap.

Sara's eyebrows knitted together with concern. She asked, "Bad dreams?"

"Yeah!" he said using the corner of the bed sheet to wipe his sweaty forehead. "As a matter of fact, that's the third time you've rescued me from a bad dream. That's including the time at the park. That was a nightmare too. Many thanks to you!" He said with a groggy voice. "This one was a doozy!"

Thinking fast was one of Sara's talents. Trying to be cheerful she said. "OK! So, this is the third time. It must be charmed 'cause look what came with it. Only the best take-out Pizza in town." She said as she rolled the table over to the bed. She flipped the lid open and displayed a pizza with everything but anchovies. She had napkins and small paper plates. "All we need now is a pitcher of cold beer but that's not a good idea with your medications. I picked up a couple of sodas from the machine on my way in.

"Ahh Man! You're an angel" He wanted to hug her. "The food here is not bad, but this is *real* food. The basics of survival." He said beaming from ear to ear. "Thank you! Ohh! This is great." He said getting out of bed and pulling on a robe. "Let's pull the table over here and sit in chairs, the beds' starting to get to me."

"I asked Doc if this idea would be OK." Sara said. "He told me that he had a feeling you would appreciate it. He also told me he would send your regular food tray to the emergency area. There's usually someone in the waiting room that would appreciate something to eat." She said picking up a slice and placed it on a plate, handing it to Carl. "I'm on lunch break so let's eat. I'm hungry. I've been smelling this pizza all the way over here. I hope it's not cooled off too much." She served herself and took a big bite.

"That's OK. Pizza's good right out if the refrigerator the next morning, hot coffee ta help ya chew the hard cheese." He said around a mouthful.

She laughed and was pleased to hear him speaking of trivial things. It was a way to get to know more about him. "I believe I'm scheduled for guard duty right outside your door tomorrow" she informed him with a smile.

"Oh good, maybe we can play cards or something." he said with delight.

"No can do. — Guard duty means I have to look out for the bad guys. Somebody *did* try to kill you, which you *don't* remember. We take this very seriously. It's possible that they might come around looking for you. We don't know if they know, that you have amnesia. They more than likely think you can identify them. Maybe they'll try to stop you any way they can." Sara said earnestly. "Could be they're trying to find out if you're alive. They must have seen the ambulance stopping after they left the park."

"We've kept this out of the papers, so far. The press has been bugging us about you. 'Who, what and where stuff,' we're considering a press-release, that says 'unknown man survives highway accident and has severe memory loss, it is believed that it is permanent because of *dain bramage*.'

To herself she said. '*OOPS!*' She thought to herself. *I did it again. Why can't I talk around this guy? Leave it alone. Don't go back to fix it.* She scolded herself for blushing.

Fussing with the pizza box, she said. "We don't believe that's such a good idea either. It's possible, they don't know where you are, or maybe they think you're dead." She served them each another piece of the pizza. "If we did, the press would be telling them exactly where you are. We're holding them back until we can find out more in the investigation." Sara said with concern.

"Mmm! Something smells good in here." Kathy said as she entered the room. "Pizza, oh my! That makes a nice early lunch."

"It *is* good. Would you like a piece?" Sara offered.

"No thanks! I just ate breakfast not too long ago. I'll put your leftovers in the refrigerator if you like." Kathy offered.

Sara and Carl looked at each other smiling and both thinking "Breakfast!"

Kathy straightened the room and bed, then left with the remaining Pizza.

Carl just sat and relaxed after Sara went back to work. He read the list from his notebook again and added.

*White van - not a memory - was told.*
*Better questions. Who wants me dead???*
*And WHY!*

Carl put the book back under the mattress. Just as he pulled his hand out the goose flesh returned to his arms. He shivered and got into the bed and pulled up the covers to ward off the chill he felt.

# SCOTT'S PLACE

"**N**obody gets high and nobody gets drunk until we figure out how to get rid of the girl." Scott said. "Who's got a plan?" He leaned back on the kitchen chair with his elbows up and his fingers locked behind his head.

Rosco said "No matter what we do it has to be *away* from *this* place. We need to dump her far away," he said as he dipped his cup in the pot for more coffee. It was really strong. Someone had put about half the jar of instant in there.

Grego was rummaging through the desk in the corner of the spare room. He found some old skin magazines, and some interesting adult toys. "Hey! Scott check this out." He shouted from the other room.

As Scott entered the room, he knew exactly what Grego had found. This after all was *his* summer bedroom. He had thought that his grandparents would have discarded that stuff by now. *Sentimental fools. At least they could have put this stuff in the basement, or something. I wonder what else they left lying around.* He wondered to himself silently. *I'll have to check the place over.*

Thinking quickly, he said aloud, "Must belong to the guy they used to rent this room to." Scott glanced around and tried with moderate success to ward off old memories that threatened to flood around him.

"Put it away for now, we've got a big problem. We've got to get rid of the girl as soon as possible." He looked at the desk again— "Look in those drawers. There might be some old maps in there somewhere. See if you can find one of this area. Oregon coast will do," he said leaving the room. "Bring it to the kitchen when you find it," Scott shouted over his shoulder. "and hurry it up!" he finished.

When Scott got to the kitchen Tuc said "Before we do anything she's got to be cleaned up — she getting ripe. She also needs to be put into a sitting position. She'll be stiff soon enough and it'll be easier to transport the body if she's sitting instead of standing or laying down." He spoke from experience.

If you knew why Tuc was in jail you would understand why Scott was impressed with him. Just looking at this light skinned Afro-American a person wouldn't think he had much savvy at all. He had a thick, wide, flat forehead above slightly crossed and widely spaced eyes. A large, sad mouth full of crooked teeth, except for the two upper front teeth. They looked like those white squares of candy-coated gum. His lips did not close in the middle without effort because of his two front teeth which were always exposed. He frequently ran his tongue over his front teeth to keep his lips from sticking to them especially when he spoke. He had formed a habit of doing this even when he wasn't speaking. His lips appeared to be slightly chapped at all times. Because of his size and his mouth being open all the time, his breathing sounded heavy and labored. People were uncomfortable around him in small areas such as elevators and in crowded rooms. They usually gave him his own space. He was physically larger than Scott's five foot eleven inches two hundred fifteen pounds. Tuc weighed in at three hundred twenty-five pounds and measured six foot, four inches tall. He was born twenty-eight years ago, with brown hair and almost gold-yellow-brown eyes. Very compelling. They draw you in, if you look in his direction too long. A child told him one time that he had robot eyes, that were made of golden metal. This made him laugh and when he smiled at him with all of his teeth showing the child ran away, too terrified to cry.

His rape victims would be left in such various positions as to appear to be reading a book *at the library*. A young couple were sitting at the *drive-in movie theater*, watching the picture with unseeing eyes. They had both been raped. One was sitting in the corner at the back *of a restaurant* with sunglasses and a meal half eaten in front of her. This is where Tucs' mind was. His little friends. He had always broken his toys as a child. He never understood how strong he was. He had broken his friends too. He had gotten very good at putting his toys back together. For some reason that he just couldn't understand. It didn't work that way with the friends that he played with sometimes. He did the best he could at putting them back together. Then leave them in a place where someone else could find them and fix them better. *Not so gentle this giant.*

Scott said. "That's a good idea, Tuc. We could take her in some bar or something through the back door. Park her in a dark corner then leave.

Grego came into the kitchen. "Scott." He waits 'til Scott looks at him then extends his arm. "Here's your map."

"Thanks"

"I was going to leave one in the rest room, sitting on the throne but they put me in jail before I could fix her. Maybe we could do that." Tuc suggested then urged the others. "We have to hurry or she'll get too stiff to work with."

Rosco came into the room after listening from the doorway. "The smell is pretty bad. It's coming out from under the door. Someone *else* has got to do the cleanup. I'm a bodyguard remember? Besides, I wasn't at the party when you guys made the mess." He turned and walked out onto the porch to get some fresh air, leaving the front door open 'cause the whole house needed some fresh air.

"OK let's all three do it." Grego said trying to, *'just get it over with'*. "It'll go a lot faster than we can get down to the serious party stuff." He said tilting his head in the direction of the loot from the drug store. "Maybe we should take some with us, so we can party after we get rid of the girl." Grego had been introduced to drugs in jail. Now he liked them very much. They all stood at the same time and went into the bedroom door. Tuc grabbed a high-backed kitchen chair, and took it with him. They held their breath and rushed to open the windows but they were painted shut. The smell was soo strong it made their eyes water. Scott sent Tuc to get the old electric fan off of the back pantry shelf but then remembered — *no electricity.*

The water and gas were turned on now so they ran some warm water in the bathtub to wash off her body. While Tuc and Grego dried her off and Scott looked through his grandmother's closet. He found a dress and scarf that would fit Sylvia just fine. It was better than trying to slide her legs back into her wet jeans. They were still wadded up on the floor by the bed. *Those will have to be thrown out.*

Tuc instructed them to put her on the chair and hold her there. He wrapped some twine and a couple of grand-pa's belts around her to hold her in place while they worked on her. They propped and tied her arms, and legs into casual positions, so that when she was completely stiff she would be in a sitting position like a live person. Because her neck was broken they secured a broom handle to her head with a scarf. She ended up looking like a hippy with an Indian headband. The sweeping end of the broom was secured to her back before they put the dress on her. Tuc also used some of grand-ma's make-up on her face, arms and legs 'cause *'her color wasn't too good'.* When he finished, he stood back looking at her and decided that all in all she didn't look bad. Just a little under the weather.

"I'm impressed, *again* Tuc." Scott said. "Gentlemen we have a man of many talents here with us." They all shared high five's with Tuc.

Tuc couldn't do anything but stand there and smile from ear to ear. If you looked closely — he was blushing a little. Scott was the only person besides his teachers that had ever paid Tuc compliments, for things that he'd done. Now everybody liked him. He was proud that they liked his work.

"OK! Let's check out this map and see where we are." Rosco said. He unfolded, scanned the map, then laid it on the table and pointed. "We are in this area here and there is a major highway about seven miles south." He pointed again, and marked the map route with a blue crayon he'd found in the drawer with the map. "We can take the highway straight to the coast. We should be able to find some out of the way rest area or something to deposit our little package in. It's the quickest route out of here and to return. What do you think?"

"Looks pretty good to me." Scott said and no one objected. "Get the stuff you want to party with and let's get on the road." Scott filled a handful of the syringes with various medications that were in the shipping box. He didn't recognize some of the names on the bottles. He grabbed some of the pills for himself. The ones he knew that he could sell in an alley somewhere if he needed money for any reason. There was only three hundred seventy-seven dollars left from the drug store, and army depot. That wasn't going to last long at the rate they were going. There were four people to feed, plus gas and oil for the truck.

Grand-pa had taken very good care of the pickup and had always told Scott that it would be his someday. Scott had found it under a tarp in the garage when they first got here. They had all gone out for a joy ride in it and then decided that they needed some different clothes to wear. On the ride one of the guys drove the 'get-away' truck that they had stolen not too far from the jail they just broke out of. They had dumped their prison wear in the back seat along with the stuff they had taken from clotheslines and laundry-mats.

They pushed the truck off the road into a vacant lot that was full of junk and overgrown with weeds tall enough to hide it. This was after they held up an army surplus depot. Only one guy in the whole place. They took clothes, shoes, guns, ammunition, and of course they each needed a fancy knife. There wasn't but forty dollars in the whole place.

They needed more money, so they held up a drugstore to get their party supplies and ended up getting something they hadn't had in a very long time. A woman. What a treat she would be. Too bad she was so fragile. They could have had lots of fun. Now because she couldn't take a good ole' healthy roll in the hey, they were out looking for a place to put her. *This is so inconvenient. Women!!!*

# TANNER'S BAR, GRILL & POOL

An hour later: They were almost to the beach. "Smell that ocean?" Tuc was asking. "I don't know about you guys, but I'm getting hungry? There's a sign that says they have the best steak sandwiches on the west coast. They have seafood too."

They sped right into a parking lot that was mostly gravel and slammed on the brakes, sending up a cloud of dust so big the it was hard to read the sign that read, "TANNERS BAR, GRILL and POOL." They stopped by the front door where Tuc and Grego jumped out of the back of the pickup.

"You go on in there and order five steak sandwiches and five cans of beer. Then you find us a place to sit by the pool table." Scott said. "I'll be in there in a minute. We're going to park out back. And don't forget to open the back door."

It was very dark in there after being out in the bright sun. They had to pause to let their eyes adjust. After a few seconds they made their way past the jukebox to the bar. They both sat at the bar on stools that were in need of new upholstery. Grego placed their order. They looked around and spotted the pool tables, (there were two) in a smaller room at the back of the bar. Grego asked the bartender if it was OK to take food into the poolroom.

"Just keep the food off the pool tables. That's all we ask." The man behind the bar answered. "Want me ta bring 'em to ya?" He asked.

"Nah! We'll com'an get 'em our own selfs." Grego mocked the bartender's accent and smiled. *It was more like a slang way of talking than an accent.* It was something that Grego did automatically. It happens without even trying. He noticed a large three-gallon jar at the end of the bar half full of pickled eggs. "Whyn-cha put 'bout five those, there eggs in a bowl an' I'll tak'em in there with the beers." Grego added and handed the man two fifty-dollar bills. "Hold on to that 'til I see if we might want sumptin' else. Say!" he said curling his finger to bring the man closer and kind of whispered. "We got a real fancy truck that we're parkin' out back, so's it doesn't get stolen or messed with. Know what I mean? Sir! Do you mind if I let ma' friends in the back door? Sir! There's only three of 'em?" He whispered all wide-eyed and innocent lookin', like he didn't want anybody else in the restaurant to hear.

"Sure fine! You'll have-ta open the door for'em though. It only opens from the inside. *Fire door* you know? I'll turn the alarm off." As long as the bartender had the two fifty-dollar bills in his hand, these guys could do whatever they liked. He flipped a switch under the counter by the cash register and disabled the alarm. He also did this whenever there was a delivery of supplies. Hell! It wasn't his Bar & Grill. He was only workin' here long enough to make trav'lin money. He's been sleeping and traveling in the small camper that he has parked out back.

The boss called him "Buddy" and that was just fine with him. The boss wouldn't be back for at least three hours. So, what if Buddy bent a few rules. Who would tell? Now he bent his efforts toward making the steak sandwiches extra special, in hopes of a good tip. These guys had money, fancy truck— They were all wearing military clothes. Probably on leave or something— traveling together.

They put Sylvia in a chair and held her up with a small table pushed into to the corner, where Tuc was fussing with her. Getting her to sit up straight. They had strapped her to the chair back with bungee cords and fastened her jacket to hide them. They started a pool game.

Buddy called out to them, "Your order's ready."

They brought it back and set one in front of Sylvia. Tuc ate half of his sandwich and placed the other half in her hands, that were propped up on the table. Then, he opened another sandwich and put mustard on it and began to eat. They enjoyed the food and even toasted Sylvia's beer can that used to be Tucs', until he traded his with hers.

They finished the beers, and ordered more food, beer and onion-rings. "The sign outside was tellin' the truth, 'cause these are the best I ever tasted." They told the bartender that military food was *nothing* compared to this. "Was he sure he hadn't worked in a fancy restaurant before he came here?"

There was a longhaired biker leaning against the doorway, watching the game and drinking a beer. He smiled when Scott looked at him. "Hi! Mind if I play the winner?" He asked Scott.

"Not at all! Just put your money on the corner of the table there." Scott said pointing with his pool stick. "M'names Harry. This is Rocko, he's Greg, that's Tank and his girl Linda, she's a little worn out from last night's party. We're trying to get her to eat before we take her home. She'll be all right though.

"I'm Carl Bridgeman," the biker said shaking Harry's hand and nodding at the others. He asked. "You guys in the service?"

"Yeah! We're on vacation for a couple of weeks. From Camp Pendleton, then we're headed south to North Carolina." Harry answered and then asked. How about you?"

"I just got laid off after 11 years with the company. They call it 'downsizing'. HA!" He hooted. "They downsized my life, so I'm taking a trip up the coast just to think things over." Carl explained.

"Sounds like a plan. Now you just drop your coins on the table and you play next winner." Harry said and thought to himself *No attachments! This is good.*

When Carl's turn came, he won easy. The guys made sure of it. They had discussed it amongst themselves while it was Carl's turn to shoot. They had all agreed that they were going to *sucker* this guy. *Let him win a couple, then bet big and make sure he loses. Bet he's got trav'lin money on him.*

# SIGNS/CLUES

Carl awoke with a start. He made his way to the bathroom and splashed cold water on his face. He was trying to take away the feelings of fear that cruised through his body with ever increasing speed. It did little for the ringing in his ears. His heart was racing It was beating faster and faster the closer he got to the bathroom. There were black spots in his vision and they multiplied until there was a dark tunnel around everything in front of him. And what he *could* see, was very far away. His vision completely disappeared. He grabbed for the edge of the sink and—.

+++++

"Carl? Carl!"

He was in bed and there was a blood pressure cuff squeezed onto his arm and someone was wiping his face with a cool cloth. "Mmmm" Carl groaned.

"His blood pressure is coming down Doc."

Carl reached up and grabbed the hand with the cloth. "Please don't make my head move. Just let it lay it still. Thank you." He peeked one eye open. Then the other. "Hey! Doc! What's happening?"

"The head nurse found you on the bathroom floor, when she was showing the new girl around. There was quite a mess, water everywhere. The sink was full and running over when they came in. It's a good thing that each bathroom has its own floor drain or we would be mopping up water out in the hallway.

"How long have I been out? Carl asked.

"Anywhere from five to forty-five minutes, maybe an hour. We don't know how long you were on the floor." Doc answered, looking at his watch while he took Carl's pulse. "You seem to be coming out of this nicely. Can you tell me what happened?"

Carl explained, "I had a dream— nightmare— that I was being held up against a wall somewhere. I was outside, and this guy stabbed me in the leg with a hypodermic syringe and pushed the plunger all the way down. Then these guys picked me up— That's when I woke up and went to wash my face."

"Do us *all* a favor son." Doc said with true concern.

What's that Doc?"

"From now on, the next time you have a bad dream, push that call button, will ya?"

Carl sighed. "OK Doc. I'll try to remember that but I was scared. I was so frightened and my heart was beating so fast. I couldn't think straight."

The two FBI agents, a few of the hospital staff, the doctor, the new girl, and his police guard were all standing around his bed.

Carl glanced at each person for a second then said. "This is embarrassing. Do you all mind if I ask for some privacy? I'd like to get out of these wet clothes. Doc would you stay a moment? Please!"

The doctor waved everybody out with his hand and told the last one to shut the door behind him. Then turned to Carl "What is it son?"

"Well, Doc. I have never said this to anyone that I can remember. I don't believe that this feeling of fear that I have is natural. I've been scared before; I know I have. This fear isn't natural, 'cause it grabs my heart and squeezes 'til I can't breathe, like if it could squeezed hard enough would pop my heart like a balloon with too much air. Does that make any sense?"

"Have you felt that there was maybe something flopping around inside your chest?" Doc asked with concern.

"Yes. Like when I was a kid and we used to chase and catch chickens. You grab their feet and their wings would beat against you. I'm afraid of this fear. I feel like it wants to kill me. Like it has its own agenda. Have you ever heard of a fear that strong before? Please Doc! Tell me you can help me." he said tearfully, pleading.

Doc smiled. "Yes, I *can* help you. First, I want you to calm down. Take some slow, deep breaths. Listen to me! Look at me!" He commanded and waited for the young man to look him in the eye. "Close your eyes if you need to."

"It's not called *fear*, it is called *anxiety*." Doc instructed "It is not natural for *anyone* to feel so anxious about life. That is why it scares you, or anyone that feels it. You're right! It's not natural, for someone living a normal life. It's only natural for a heart to react like that when some part of you is in trouble. It's a warning sign. With your loss of memory, it's a wonder to me that you haven't shown signs of anxiety before this. Actually, I'm glad to finally see that you're reacting like this. It shows me that your natural defenses are kickin' in. Your body is telling you that it needs help. Something is wrong.

"That's good news doc. I didn't know what to think about it. Maybe like something evil was inside me. Messin' with my mind", Carl said patting his chest with an open palm.

"Our bodies tell us what they need, if only we knew how to listen. That is what doctors do. We look at and listen to the warning signs, and only then do we know what to do. When your body needs fuel, you feel hungry. When your body needs warmth, you get a chill. With you, you need to remember something about your past that's very important. That hasn't happened yet, so your body feels anxious. I'm going to give you a tranquilizer for now instead of the sedative you've been getting. If this is truly what your body needs, it should help your headaches too. They could be stress headaches. I'll send the nurse in with something right away." Before Dr. Handle turned to leave the room, he asked. "Is there anything else I can do for you right now?"

"No. That's all. Thanks! I feel much better just talking about it." Carl said, as he leaned back and closed his eyes. "I was starting to feel like I was losing it. It helps big time to know that somebody else understands. Thanks!"

Doc opened the door and stepped out of the room. The police guard and the FBI agents confronted him. "What's going on doctor? Is he going to be all right?"

"Yes, yes he'll be fine. I believe any one of us would have anxiety too if we couldn't remember who we are, or why we ended up in the hospital. He just needs time, he'll be fine. Excuse me gentlemen." He pressed past their expectant faces, and headed to the nurses' station to order Carl's medication.

The twins were at the station when he got there. Crystal said "We were just informed that Carl had a problem a little while ago." Then she asked noting the concern on Doc's face. "Do you think it wise, to go forward with this afternoon's session?"

"I think whatever you do will help him. He is suffering from the frustrations, and the anxieties of his memory loss. It's hard to imagine his sense of loss. If he learns anything at all from this session, it will be of benefit to him. I'd like you to wait for this. It's a tranquilizer instead of his usual medication." Doc said and handed Ruby the prescription. "You can give it to him, before you get started. It will probably help things go a little smoother. I'll enter it on his chart, just make sure you initial it, when you get through." He said, then excused himself.

The twins stopped by the hospital pharmacy for the tranquilizer before they went to see Carl. On their way to his room, they shared thoughts about what they would try to do today. They were both anticipating good results. They both knew that Carl was a special person. There was a positive response from just about everyone that came in contact with him.

As the twins approached the room, the two FBI agents stood at attention. The girls did that to people. There was just something magnetic about them. They were both beautiful in their own individual ways. The combination of Crystals almost straight, white blond hair swaying and bouncing almost to her waist, rippling like a cascading waterfall as she walked, and Ruby's strawberry blond, wavy hair cascading down her back and rippling when she walked as if it were liquid, was awesome. Quite often people would stop talking and sometimes even arguing to watch them walk by. It sent the average man into thoughts of magic, wizardry and fantasy. They would stumble all over themselves trying to be manly and polite. The twins were in civilian clothes today, which was always magic to anyone laying eyes on them. Whether it be man, woman or child. There are certain children that call them 'The Angel Ladies'. Their auras were spectacular to anyone that could see them, especially when the two were together, which was most of the time. Normally, when they were at work, they were in uniform and had their hair confined to hair clips, bobby pins and nurses caps. They were very professional in appearance, nothing too far out of the ordinary. Just two very beautiful women.

Letting their hair out of artificial confines, enlarged their auras. When they were together, their combined strengths and talents were awesome. Almost like angels with wings no one would go against them.

"Hello Ladies! May *I* help you." One of the FBI men asked, standing in front of the other. The other one said looking over his partners' shoulder. "Yes, ladies how may *we* help you?" As he sidestepped the other to get in front of him.

"Well for one thing, you can stand aside. Neither one of you have the authority to block this door." Ruby said. One of their talents was putting anyone out of place, back into their place with little or no effort.

As the agents stepped on each other's feet trying to get out of the way, the girls stepped past them. They both walked over to the police guard and took turns giving him a hug and a kiss on his cheek. Crystal whispered in his ear. "Steven, don't tell these guys were cousins, just let 'em burn." As she stepped away from him, he winked and said loud enough for them to hear, "You got it sweetheart." Then he winked at Ruby, and she air kissed him. The girls disappeared into the room as the two FBI agents just stood there with their mouths open, which automatically increased the size of Steven's smile.

The twins closed the door behind them. Carl was sitting in one of his chairs, reading his notebook. He looked up and smiled. He couldn't help himself. He was not affected like the agents outside his door. They were beautiful but he also felt their warmth and compassion. They were his lifeline. He knew that if anyone could help him, these two women would do it. He had no doubts. They gave him a feeling confidence and he had no fear of *what they do.*

Alternately they both greeted him.

"Good morning to both of you."

"Let's try 'good afternoon." Crystal said and Ruby chimed in. It's after one o'clock." They both smiled, and that warmed his heart. He felt only the slightest apprehension but stronger than that was excitement. This afternoon there was a new feeling of confidence that warmed him. Not a whole lot but he felt it getting stronger. It felt kind of natural to be dealing with things of the mind. He knew without asking that this was the way to find his answers and questioned nothing they did. As if it were not uncommon at all — looking up and seeing angels. *This is supposed to be,* he told himself and it felt good to think that way. *This is a good thing.*

Ruby spoke first. "I'd like you to be in the bed for this session. You need to be reclined and relaxed."

"Oh sure!" he said and headed for the bed, dropping the notebook on the table. He spotted the small tray containing the syringe and automatically rolled up his sleeve for the injection.

Ruby picked the notebook up and fingered the cover.

Carl climbed up onto the bed, making himself comfortable and he used the controls to raise the head of the bed a little.

Crystal injected the medication and said, "Before we go to the next level, Carl close your eyes and hold out your hands, palms upward, both of them together please. I'm going to put your wallet in your hands. Do not open it yet. I want you to close all thoughts out of your mind, accept what comes to you through touching your wallet. You've had contact with it for the last seven and a half years. Let your fingers travel on the surface." Crystal Counseled.

"Mmm! There's too much here. It's confusing." Carl said shaking his head slowly.

Crystal sandwiched Carl's hands and the wallet between her own, and calmed his anxieties. After a few moments she said, "We know that this wallet was not with you when you lost your memory. That is a fact. You left it at the bar before getting on your motorcycle. This is not the proper time to explore the wallet. Please, hand the wallet back to me and do not think about it right now. That will come after we get past the chemical barrier. I'm sure that you will have many stories to tell, after the wall comes down."

"I'm ready if you are." Carl handed the wallet back to Crystal, and she put it on the table, with the notebook.

The twins looked at each other while Ruby handed Carl a note.

It read: Escalator.

"Don't forget! You must bring your thoughts to the surface, before you can share them. Now. Look for the first thing that makes itself known."

Carl stepped onto the escalator and was immediately with friends, at the place where he used to work. "I'm thanking Sally, Jerry, Jim for the going away party." He said aloud and looked down in his hand and saw his layoff notice. "I've been laid off from my job, after eleven years." He said with bitter sadness. A tear formed in the corner of his eye.

"Look at the paper in your hand, and tell me your name and the date." Crystal said.

He read the form. He said "My name is Carlton F. Bridgeman and the date is March 24, 1995."

Ruby asked "What is the name of the company and how do you feel about this?"

"Howard's Aircraft Company, and I am relieved in a way. It was a 'go nowhere' job. I could do this job for the next twenty or thirty years. Nothing would change. You do the same thing day after day, nothing. Good-bye, thanks again. It's Friday night and the gang wants to take, me and four other guys that got their pink slips, out for a few drinks. This is the last time we're going to see each other after all these years," he said drifting out of context.

Ruby instructed as she put the 'Nerf' ball back in his hand. "Here's your control handle. Let's go down to the next level. Remember it has feather touch control, you don't have to squeeze it very hard.

"Where are you now Carl?" Crystal asked. "Why are you packing your clothes? Are you going somewhere?"

"I just sold my dirt bike. Got Seven hundred eighty dollars. I only rode it four times, but I need the money for the trip."

"What trip is that Carl?" Crystal asked.

"I need to get away from Los Angeles. I'm going nowhere in this place. There's too much pressure to be like everybody else. It's unreal."

"I'm going to drive my motorcycle up the coast. I need to think about absolutely *nothing* for a while and then hopefully I'll know what I want to do with my life. First, I'll clear out all the cobwebs that have collected since I started that job." He paused a few seconds. "Once you get into that life, it's like there is no other world. You can't survive without the company. They make you a dependent and you like it at first. Good money coming in and before you know it, when you even think you want out you can't because your lifestyle demands that you make the money you do to maintain the status quo. It runs your life, tells you when to sleep, what to eat, what to wear, and worst of all they force you to be there. They bleed you for all of your ideas and claim them for themselves. They put you up against a ruler and tell you that you don't get a raise if you don't continually improve and give, give, give to the company for the *good of everybody*. Yeah! Everybody in the upper offices, AKA: *Mahogany Row*. That's what sucks about big business. They survive by eating the souls of the little guys." Carl stopped talking, smiled and said. "I'm out of there and thanks. Laying me off was the best thing that could have happened to me. That's in the past. They're not going to munch on my soul anymore."

Ruby made a mental note that these facts were very important to him because he showed such strong feelings. With the release from the anchor created by his old job, he truly was feeling a newly born freedom.

He squeezed the handle hard and was immediately in a deli. He said "I'm buying food to eat when I get to the camp site. I'm traveling up the coast and I'm stopping off at public camping areas. No hotels. They cost too much and there's too many people around. If you're in a motel and you want to sing or shout at the top of your lungs, they call the cops, *because you must be crazy.*

"I got everything tied down on my bike, nice and tight with bungee cords, and I'm on the road again.

Crystal asked. "What's a bungee cord?"

Carl showed them both the elastic ropes that secured his belongings to the backrest on the bike. He told them that — "Sometimes these are called 'Shock Cords' but mostly they are referred to as 'Bungee Cords.' They have a hook on each end. They can secure just about anything, without tying and untying knots."

He squeezed the handle softly this time and was riding his bike on a lazily curving road that was lined on both sides with Pine, Oak and Spruce trees. There were about twenty curbside style mailboxes all in a row, on posts at the side of the road. Without them, one would never know that people lived here. Their driveways were small gravel roads that seem to disappear into the bushes. You could miss these if you didn't know what they were or weren't looking for them.

"There's a sign, it says TANNER'S BAR, GRILL and POOL." Carl pointed at the sign. His motions made it possible for the girls to see it too. He said. "It'll be nice to hear some music before I turn in for the night. My portable radio needs batteries. They're too expensive at the deli. I'm going to park out back so that nobody spots my stuff and messes with it."

The twins step inside with him.

He's at the bar. He pulls out his wallet so he doesn't have to stand up again to get it out of his back pocket. He lays the wallet and a ten on the bar and orders a beer. He picks up the change and his beer and walks over to the jukebox, puts some coins in and selects some music. He hears the click of the balls on a pool table and turns to see the poolroom. He walks over to watch the game in progress. He leans against the doorway.

*These guys must be in the service. They were all wearing military camouflage clothing.* He asks, after being spotted in the doorway. "Mind if I play winners?"

One of the guys comes over holding his hand out, real friendly like.

Not at all! Just put your money on the corner of the table, there." Scott said pointing. M'names Harry. This is Rocko. He's Greg. That's Tank and his girl Linda. She's a little worn out from last night's party. We're trying to get her to eat, she'll be all right.

"I'm Carl Bridgeman," he announced, sticking out his own hand to shake Harry's and nodding at the others. "You guys in the service." More of a statement than a question of what appeared to be obvious.

"Yeah! We're on vacation for a couple of weeks. From Camp Pendleton, then we're headed south to North Carolina." Harry answered and then asked. How about you?"

"I just got laid off after 11 years with the company. They call it 'downsizing'. They downsized my life so I'm taking a trip up the coast just to think things over." Carl explained.

"Sounds like a plan. Now you just drop your coins on the edge of the table and you can play next winner." Harry said returning to his game.

Carl won the first game, really easily. He thought to himself. *These guys aren't very good pool players.* When he won the second game, the guy named Greg started to get upset. "What are you some kind of pool shark? Why are you hustling us? Who do you think you are anyway?"

Carl looked around. The friendly guy, Harry was nowhere in sight, I guessed that he took the girl outside for some fresh air. So, he had to handle these guys himself. Tank, the big guy with the bad teeth, *Hum! I thought the service had a good dental plan.* was getting in his face, about cheating, using tricks. "You can't fool me." Tank was almost shouting.

The bartender was at the doorway, telling them "You're going to have to take any arguments outside. The other customers were complaining about the rowdy noise."

Greg says, "OK fella let's go outside."

Tank grabs Carl's arm, and pulls him towards the back door then pushed him through the door into the parking lot behind the bar. What Carl saw made his heart skip a beat. "Oh! No, no! I'd forgotten about this." He was frightened and started breathing hard. Then his heart started pounding inside his chest like he had just ran around the block.

Ruby said. "It's OK Carl, they can't hurt you. Breathe slowly. — Deeper, that's it — relax. Breathe.

Crystal added. "This guy scares me too but think of it as a movie that we've already seen and we are just watching the rerun so we can remember what happens. These are only memories. No one can hurt you. Ruby and I are your guides, we will pull you back from harm. Now let's find out what happened to you. Step back on the escalator right where you stepped off. We need to know what happened in the parking lot. Ready?" she asked.

With quick short strokes Carl nodded his head and closed his eyes. "Let's go."

They were back in the parking lot. Ruby suggested that he look at what was happening to him from outside his body as if he were a spectator. As she said that, his mind clutched the idea like a lifeline. The three of them were watching together.

Carl was being dragged out of the bar; they saw Harry eating a sandwich made of the things that were on Carl's bike. The rest of Carl's things were all over the ground. His saddlebags were open, the straps were cut and the padlocks were still locked to the straps that hung down. They also saw the girl setting on the bike. She was still wearing the sunglasses that she'd had on inside the bar. Carl had not seen until right now, that there was a broom handle tied to the back of the girl's head. The headscarf she was wearing also encompassed the handle. This kept her head from flopping around on her broken neck.

The twins had no control of what was happening. Ruby asked to get closer to the girl and Carl obliged. Stop! Ruby said. Don't get too close. I found out what I need to know. The girl is dead. They've strapped her to your bike with those bungee cords of yours. They are planning to blame you, for her death. They were probably thinking that those cords would come off during the accident, you were bound to have. You have been blaming yourself, now you know that you don't have to.

Crystal asked to pull back a little from the girl. "We need to concentrate on Carl. Look at this."

Carl was being pushed up against the outside wall, next to the bar's back door.

Carl says "This is my nightmare."

"Easy does it" the twins assured. "We're just watching."

Harry stuck a syringe into the girls arm right through her jacket then he was headed toward Carl, he said. "Don't worry I saved this one for you." He was pulling something out of his jacket pocket and used his thumb to pop the plastic shield off of the needle. It was another syringe, and it had liquid in it too. Without hesitation Harry stabbed Carl in the leg, right through his pants and pushed the plunger all the way down. Harry grinned at Carl and told him. "Now if you're careful enough, and fast enough there's a hospital down the road about three miles. You might make it in time to save both of you.

Carl asked, "What kind of crazy bastard are you anyway?

Harry answered. "Ah! Ah! Ah! Let's have none of that childish crap out of you. You're wasting time. You'd better hurry. Harry reached past Carl and pushed the starter button, and the bike roared to life. The two big guys picked Carl up while Greg guided Carl's legs putting one over the seat. They placed Carl's hands on the handlebars and pushed the bike off of the kickstand. Harry squeezed Carl's hand tight against the clutch handle and used his foot to pop the bike into gear. "Now go boy! Go! You still have time."

The bike and riders pulled unsteadily out of the parking lot and turned right onto the road. It weaves wildly around the curves. There was a pickup truck following the bike. Two guys in the cab and two guys standing in the back looking over the cab, cheering him on. "Better go faster you'll never make it in time. Faster! Faster!" They taunted loudly. There was a steep hill leading down toward the main highway. You had to turn either left or right because the ocean was straight ahead, about forty feet, on the other side of the wooden four-by-four guard rail, and down the cliff on the other side.

As Carl neared the bottom of the hill, the drug was taking affect. He didn't have much control of the bike at all and was just hanging on for the ride of his life. Everything was going in slow motion. He was going too fast to make the turn, but in his drugged state of mind he thought he was going to make it. He miscalculated the angle he needed to lean the bike to make the turn. Everything was mixed up. His vision was swimming around unnatural, nothing was logical or where it should be. He needed to get to the hospital or they would die. He didn't even know this girl. The bike laid down instead of just leaning. The bike was now laying down and sliding on its side towards the far side of the highway and the railing. Because of the bikes speed, the parts of the bike that were in contact with the pavement were throwing sparks into the air. In a matter of seconds, it slid past the pavement and onto the dirt. Carl was bent over, standing on and riding the bike like it was a surfboard. The bike lurched over the little guardrail and Carl just stepped off the bike as it kept going, right on down, out of sight.

He shook his head, and when his vision cleared and his thoughts came back to his head he found himself looking down at his left heel perched on the edge of a cliff.

His vision telescoped to the waves crashing on the rocks below. His heart stumbled in his chest and beat loudly in his ears. Each beat seemed to lean him ever so slightly towards the edge. The breath froze in his lungs so suddenly that he felt dizzy. He asked himself, "Have I been holding my breath?"

The only part of him that seemed to function were his eyelids. All he could do was close them and pray that this is a dream. As darkness closed on his vision, he said aloud, "Dear God help me please! Please help me!" He felt cold wind caress his back.

Being afraid that his heart and the wind would push him over the edge, he leaned back into the air. It felt like a giant pillow that touched every inch of his backside, pushing ever so gently. He was afraid to lift either foot, for fear the wind would pick him up and cast him out into the air. He dug his heels in, leaned back and felt as if he were gently lowered to the ground behind him.

+ + + + +

Five minutes later: Ruby was wiping his sweat beaded head with a cold cloth.

Crystal was sitting in a chair next to the bed. She said, "I feel like I've been to the horror movies played in 3-D." She reached up and touched Carl's hand. "It's over. You don't have to do that ever again."

Carl placed his hand over hers and looked at Ruby. "The pickup truck. I've seen it right outside this window. And, I'm sure I recognize the passengers. Thomas and I were watching the two men in it, arguing just yesterday. The guy with the cast on his arm dropped something in the hall. Then he nodded at me on his way to the door."

"Yes!" Ruby said. "I remember helping him. He dropped his medication or some kind of medical supplies. I picked it up for him. I didn't get any bad vibes from him. I can usually tell right away by touching something that the person was holding. Maybe it hadn't been in his possession very long."

# SCOTT'S ADVENTURE

They were following the bike, down the curved road towards the coast. The pavement was a little slippery from the sand that had washed across the road in the recent rain. They were all howling and hollering when the bike laid down and clamored across the highway making sparks fly in all directions.

"Yah Hooo! What a show" Scott said. "Check it out. He's riding that thing like a damn surfboard, man! It looks like we got rid of that probl— Hey! He didn't go over. Look-it that. He's crawling away from the cliff.

The truck fishtailed into the four-by-four railing sideways and Tuc was pitched out of the back end when the tires on one side of the truck dipped into the dirt. It tipped sideways and then bounced back onto all four tires.

"Oh! Boy are we in the shit now. Look! There's people stopping." Rosco said from the driver's seat.

Scott jumped out of the truck and checked on Tuc. He was dirty but not hurt except for a couple scratches. "Com'on help me get this guy in the truck."

There was a man walking towards them. "You need any help there? I've got some first aid in the car."

Scott shouted back to him, above a mild wind that had come up. "Nah he'll be OK. We're taking him to the medical center just down the road a piece. It'll be faster. But, thanks anyway! That's very kind of you."

"Wasn't there somebody on the back of that bike?" The 'Good Samaritan' asked.

"What?" Scott asked. Then realizing that the guy saw the girl. He added quickly. "Naw! That was just his sleeping bag, bedroll and some other stuff. He just left our place. He's headed out on a camping trip with his family."

Scott and Tuc put Carl in the back of the truck and got in with him. Scott said "Grego, you sit up front and tell Rosco to get us the hell out of here."

Rosco drove the truck right back up the hill, and past the 'TANNERS' BAR, GRILL AND POOL' establishment. He kept driving for about twenty minutes, and then pulled over to the side of the road. Rosco and Grego got out of the truck and walked to the back end, leaned over the side of the truck and looked at Carl. Grego says, "How come he's all rolled up into a ball like that?

"Probably the drug." Scott volunteered. "We don't know what most of that stuff is or what it will do."

Grego was getting very nervous and asked. "What do you think Scott? Tuc? Rosco? Anybody? Come on you guys. We can't just sit here. What are we going to do?"

Tuc said, "We got'ta get different transportation, a van maybe. Have any of you guys seen a sign pointing to a town around here? We need to find a car dealer."

Nobody asked why or how, they just got back in the truck and drove. Carl was covered with the trucks tarp while they drove around. Nobody wanted anyone in the taller vehicles seeing inside the back of the truck. They turned onto the road and followed signs to a dealership about ten miles inland from the beach. Scott told Rosco "Pull over about half a block before we get there. Try to find something to park behind like a truck or a bush, tree anything. Just not out in the open. When you see us coming, follow, OK???"

They parked next to a trash dumpster that was at the curb waiting for a garbage truck. Scott and Grego tucked in their shirts, straightened out themselves best that they could, walked into the dealership parking lot and started checking out the utility vans. *Just plain with no windows in the back.* The salesman was right there, eager to make a sale. "May I help you gentlemen?" he asked.

Scott said "I've never driven a van before. My friend here told me that they are no different than a car. Is that true?" Before the little man could answer Scott said, "See, I want to move some of my stuff down to Texas and I'd rather do it myself than paying someone to do it for me, and—."

Following Scott's example of interrupting, the salesman jumped into the conversation and said, "Well my man, there's one way to find out. Let me go get the keys and we can take it for a spin. "I'll be right back."

Grego shouted after him. "Thanks, that's very kind of you."

Scott said. "Don't be too thankful. It might sound funny. He's supposed to go get the keys." he said gesturing with his hands. *"He's trying to sell the van to us.* Remember? Anyway, I guess the little guy is nervous or maybe he's just anxious to make a sale 'cause he never introduced himself. The van is ours."

Sorry! OK! I'm just a little nervous too and I'm still shook up about what happened a little while ago.

While Scott and Grego were getting the van, Carl started to wake up. He groaned and began to unroll.

Being afraid that someone would see him in the back of the truck if he sat up, Tuc hit him up-side his head with a foot long piece of one-inch metal water pipe that had been rolling around in the bed of the pickup. It took about three or four thumps before Carl fell over on his side and lay still, *unconscious again.* Tuc wondered to himself. *I hope I didn't break him. I just wanted him to be quiet.*

Rosco yelled through the window at Tuc. "Hold on, here they come." They followed the white van until it had stopped about three miles down the road. It had pulled over next to a car wrecking yard. The kind that you 'pick the part' you want. You just roam around until you find what you want, take it off the wrecked car, show the cashier what you have, and pay for it. The pickup stayed on the street.

The van drove around in the wrecking yard, *'looking for parts.'* When they got to a spot that couldn't be seen from the front office, it stopped. The car dealer was deposited in the trunk of an old wreck that no one would be pickin' parts off of, 'cause it had been totaled, even the door handles were bent out of shape. It took them a good three to four minutes to get the trunk open.

Scott had asked for Rosco to test drive the van, 'cause he knows more about vans than I do.' The salesman was more than willing to let either one of them test drive. He just wanted to make a sale. Scott had grabbed and pulled the little man right between the front seats. He stuck a syringe in his neck and held him until he passed out. Then he injected the man two more times with the empty syringe, injecting air directly into the man's heart, *just to be sure* he told himself. *'cause he didn't know what this stuff was. It might be just vitamins for cryin' out loud.*

Before they pulled out of the wrecking yard, they opened the side doors to show the cashier the empty van. They hadn't stolen anything — they just didn't find the part they were looking for. "Thanks anyway." They headed for the road again, with the pickup following. As Scott had instructed, they headed for the industrial area that they spotted on the way to the car dealership. The van stopped next to an old building and opened the side doors facing towards the wall. The pickup pulled up between the wall and the van, with the truck bed adjacent to the open van doors.

Carl was still coiled up in a ball. His muscles were hard and tight and held him in that position. "What's with this guy? All balled up like that." Grego asked, and added, "It's not natural. Don't all your muscles get loose when you're passed out like that? "Where did the blood on his head come from? Did he get that from the bike accident?"

Tuc said that he had to quiet him 'cause he started waking up'.

Scott said. "I already told you it's probably the drug. How do I know? I ain't no doctor."

Rosco and Tuc had to pick Carl up and lift him out so that Scott and Grego could kind of grab and roll him into the van. There were no seats, just carpeting on the floor and paneling on the walls and back door. He was a difficult bundle to manage. He was about as big as Scott, at almost six foot tall.

Scott took his belt off, looped it under the back of Carl's belt, then through the spare tire wheel that was mounted to the side wall by the back doors and buckled it closed. This was to keep Carl from rolling around in the back of the van.

"Hey! Listen up." Scott had everyone's attention while he gave instructions. "This is what we're going to do. Rosco and I are going to follow the van. Grego will be driving, with Tuc in the back. Grego, I need you to drive up there." He pointed toward the hills. "We are going to be following in the pickup." I want you to go up in the hills until you get to a place where you can push this guy here out, so he'll roll down a *long* hill. We need him to roll, slide or whatever, a *long way down* from the road so that he can't be seen too good from the top if somebody were to be hiking or walking by. Make sure it's a steep hill. OK?"

Tuc and Grego both nodded in agreement.

"You may not see us right behind you, but we'll be coming up a little way back. In case of trouble, you guys can jump out and get in the pickup"

It took them almost an hour to get into the hills. They were at a greater distance than it looked to be. They wound around curves left and right while increasing their altitude for about thirty or forty-five more minutes. Grego was getting uneasy about the amount of time it was taking. He wanted to just dump this guy anywhere to get rid of him. Besides that, he was getting hungry again. Tuc had said that he was hungry before they even started this trip up the hill, but Scott nixed that until the body was gone.

"Hey my friend, ya know this makes three bodies now?" Grego said to Tuc over his shoulder, holding up three fingers. "Scott's getting stranger by the hour. He does the killing and we do the cleaning up, just like he tells us to do. I'm getting a really bad feeling about this. I never liked being around Scott that much in the first place. Let's just do this now and get it over with. There's a curve ahead with a wide shoulder we can pull over on. Open the door. I'll slow down while you push this guy out. Wait 'til I get close to the edge. I'll say 'NOW'. Then, you push. OK?"

"Right! Good plan my friend. What you been thinkin' is right too." Tuc said as he cut the belt that held Carl in place. He loved using his brand-new knife. Scott might be pissed 'cause he don't have a belt now. So what? *Mmm! That heavy thick leather belt cut like it was made out of soft butter.* He admired the blade as he closed the knife and then slid it in his pocket. Tuc slid the door open and leaned back on his elbows, bent his knees, put both of his feet on Carl, and waited Grego's signal.

Grego pulled off the road on to the shoulder, raising a dust cloud as he applied the brakes. The van swerved a little and Grego yelled, "NOW! PUSH NOW."

Tuc pushed hard by straightening his legs quickly. He had to grab the doorframe to keep himself inside the van. Grego spun the tires in the gravel and then they caught the pavement. Tuc managed with some difficulty to slide the side door closed and then worked his way up to the front seat. He said looking out at the passenger side rearview mirror. "There's another vehicle behind us."

As Grego headed for the road, he looked in the driver's side rearview mirror. "Oh damn! There's an ambulance behind us and it's stopping. Damn! Damn! Damn! Of all the luck," he said pounding on the steering wheel with his fist. "Scott's going to be pissed now. I hate it when he gets crazy. Oh! Man! Damn!", he yelled above the van's engine.

Just then the pickup passed them in its own cloud of dust. Scott was waving his arm out the window, in a signal that meant 'Follow! — Hurry up!'

When Grego looked down at the speedometer, he was only going twenty-five miles per hour. He stepped on the gas and caught up with the truck. They followed it to a wide spot in the road where it stopped. They parked behind it. Scott jumps out and walked over to the van on the passenger side. He had a blue vein enlarged and pulsating down the middle of his forehead. He bent down and leaned on the window's frame and said. "We have to get rid of this van. We need to drive out of this area, follow me." He spun on one foot and stomped back to the truck, but before he got in, he turned and looked at Grego.

"Damn! Did you see the way he looked at me?" With Tuc nodding his head they just looked at each other and followed the pickup silently. No talking, no radio. They went higher into the hills until they found a freeway sign. They headed west and before they got to the freeway, saw a sign that read.

## CAR POOL - PARK AND RIDE
## NEXT TWO EXITS
## CALL 1-800-NO-STRESS

They followed the truck into the parking lot. There was an area for weekly/monthly parking where the van pulled in, between two other vans.

Scott motioned for them to get into the back of the pickup without speaking.

Tuc and Grego silently moved to the back of the truck.

+++++

Rosco drove the truck back to the house, while Scott fumed in the passenger seat. By the time they got home, Scott was calmer but remained silent. He went into the bedroom, pulled the sheets off the bed, flipped the soiled mattress over, flopped face down on it and stayed there. After about fifteen minutes Rosco knocked on the door and entered without waiting for an answer. "We're going for hamburgers; can we get you something?"

"What's the matter with the stuff that's left over? We didn't eat it *all* last night. Did we?" Scott said rolling over onto one elbow with the palm of his hand on the side of his head.

Rosco answered. "There's no electricity, some spoiled and rats got to most of the rest.

"Rats? Oh damn! We're going to have to make another *loan* soon." Scott said looking in his wallet. He pulled out three twenties and handed them to Rosco. "I'll have a couple cheeseburgers, large order onion rings, two fries and two chocolate shakes. Take Grego with you, I'm not ready to talk to him yet. See if you can find a seven-eleven, a store or something and pick up some extra toilet paper, trash bags the black kind. Get enough to cover all the windows on the inside, and a couple rolls of three-inch masking tape. Some cold beers and chips for later, maybe some dip too, bean, salsa, — whatever."

Rosco made a list so he wouldn't forget anything. After he left, Scott cleaned up the entire mess that Sammy had made. He always cleaned up after Sammy. He didn't mind, 'cause he and Sammy always made each other feel good. He loved Sammy, even if he did have a bad temper and hurt other people. Scott took his grandparents portrait into the bathroom to clean it off. He had used toilet paper and water before. After twenty minutes it finally came clean. *I got'ta do this before it dries,* he reminded himself. The paint was wearing thin from all the cleaning. He stuck the nail back in the hole and hung the portrait back on the wall.

Somebody knocked and said through the door. "Foods here."

Scott yelled back. "Be right there." He headed for the kitchen and found the group had already unpacked the food bags. "Oh good! I'm starving. Thanks for going."

Rosco had set all of Scott's food at the end of the table including two of the chocolate shakes. He got his own food and went into the living room. He turned on his portable television. He had lifted it off the security desk at the military depot. It was on the guards' desk just talking to itself. The man wouldn't need it anymore. Scott had seen to that the minute they walked through the door. If he had only waited, the guard could have told them that there was a floor-safe with over seven thousand dollars in it. Scott was on the guy and had snapped his neck before he could speak. He had always been the type of guy that jumped in with both feet before finding how deep it was. Grand-pa told him many times too, *'Think about what you're doing first son or you're going to end up hurt real bad someday'.* Scott always put it off as *'old man talkin' — what could he know?'*

The television was propped up on its stand, sitting on the coffee table. It had a three-inch screen with a color picture. Within five minutes the other guys were leaning towards the television, watching the tiny screen. Rosco was flipping through the channels looking for the local news. The television was picking up about five channels good enough to see and hear well. There was nothing about Carl or the salesman or even the missing van. Rosco turned the TV off and put it back in his jacket pocket, and said "I'll try again later, for some news. Sorry, have to save the batteries until I can get some more. The portable radio we got from the biker needs batteries too." Rosco slurped the last of his coke while he told Scott the other stuff was in the bedroom.

"Good! Thanks." Scott said and told everybody, "We're going to have to split the trash bags open and tape them to the windows. I don't want any light coming through the windows while we're here. It might be seen from the road."

Tuc said, "There's no electricity, Scott. How's the light supposed shine through the windows?"

Scott instructed. "There will be light if you go into the shed out back. You'll find candles and lanterns. Why don't you do that? There's a key in the junk drawer, next to the kitchen door. It's got brown paint on it that matches the shed." This was something that his grandmother did to teach him when he was young. The front door key had green paint that matched the front porch steps. "Grego see if you can help him. OK?"

"Sure! Your grandparents were prepared for anything like emergencies and stuff, weren't they? They're pretty smart. That's probably where you got your smarts from, huh Scott?

Scott stared at the little man until Grego lowered his eyes. He knew that Grego was just trying to appease him, with what was thought to be a compliment. Scott held Sammy in check by telling him not to be upset with Grego, that he — Scott, would take care of the little man tomorrow. He said to Grego, "You'd be surprised at the things they were prepared for. Now, go along with Tuc and make sure he can find what we need." Scott said kindly.

After Grego left the room he shivered physically with goose bumps that raised the hair on the back of his neck. When he and Tuc got to the shed he told the big man that he was afraid. He knew just by the look in the man's eyes that he — Scott had a punishment planed for him because he screwed up in front of the ambulance today. He hadn't seen the vehicle until it was too late.

Tuc pulled out a lighter and lit it so they could search for a candle. It was dark in the shed.

Grego took one of the candles and set it up in an empty ashtray that was on one of the shelves. While they searched for and found what they needed, Grego told Tuc that he didn't like the look in Scott's eyes and that he was really frightened *'cause you know how he gets'*. Before he goes crazy, he gets really nice and kind. We've both seen him like this before. He's nuts in the head. Now he's pissed off at me."

Tuc reached out to put his arm around Grego to comfort him. Because of Tucs' height, his arm only encircled Grego's head. He pulled him towards his chest and said, "Don't worry little buddy, I won't let him kill ya. . ." He held the little man away from him so that he could see his face, and with a teasing smile said, . . . very much!" He bent over and hugged the little man, like a doll, lifting Grego's feet off the floor as he straightened to a standing position. "You can sleep next to me tonight if you're worried. OK?" he said protectively, patted Grego's butt and released him gently to the floor holding one of the little man's arms until he was steady on both feet.

"Thanks, Tuc, I really appreciate it. We better get back in the house, *before* anything can go wrong. Let's keep him happy tonight, maybe we can get a good night's sleep. Thank you, my good friend. Now! Please help me carry these things into the house."

+++++

The next morning everyone was well rested. Rosco got up early and went to a Seven-Eleven and got stuff for everybody's breakfast. Readymade Egg muffins with sausage patty, bagels, cream cheese, strawberry jam and some more instant coffee. Before he left, he put on a big pot of water to boil. When he got back it was boiling. He made coffee and called everybody to breakfast. Again, he watched the news. Still nothing that concerned them. Not even the jailbreak. Something strange was going on.

+++++

After everyone had eaten and they were all gathered in the living room Scott said. "We need to find out if Carl survived *and* can he talk. Anybody got any ideas? Come on let's hear what you guys been thinkin' about our situation here. I know it's been on everybody's mind, we're in this together. Do I have to do all the thinking?"

Everybody knew that Scott had already decided what they were going to do, but he just wanted to tell them that their ideas won't work after they said what they thought. Everybody thought it was his way of telling himself that he was better than the rest. In reality it was Sammy that needed the ego boost but nobody knew about Sammy. To keep Scott in a good mood, they would all tell him that *his* was the best idea of all and they'll do what he says. "That's the *best* idea."— "Scott you always have the *best* ideas."— "I don't know why we even bother telling you anything that *we* might have thought of."— "*You're* the smartest guy around."

*This* time though, Scott hadn't told them what his plans were, Sammy had his own ideas.

It always boosted Scott's ego when the guys showed their support.

Sammy was getting stronger like, before they went to jail. So— for a short time he would have to let Sammy take over. Scott always got a really bad headache when he tried to keep Sammy quiet. When he was in jail, they had pills to keep the pain away. He couldn't bring them with him because they only let him have one at a time, and they kept the bottle in the infirmary. They always made sure he swallowed it too. There wasn't anything that he could use in the stuff they got from the pharmacy. He didn't even think to look for the stuff *he needed*, while they were there. Sammy had kept his mind busy doing other things. Scott doesn't think that Sammy likes the medication, 'cause he refuses to talk to Scott after he takes it.

Grego needed to be reprimanded for his stupidity yesterday. Scott was not much for dealing out the punishments. So, he would get Grego outside and let Sammy take care of him. Then he would have to make sure that Sammy rested for a while. Sammy always gets tired easily. Being angry uses up a lot of his energy.

"Grego, I need some help with the pickup." Scott told him. "Come on out-side, I'll show you what to do

"OK boss." Grego cringed, and looked at Tuc as the goose flesh crawled up his arms.

Tuc said under his breath. "Go on. I'll watch from the window. If he tries to get rough, I'll be out there in a flash. Go now, before he gets angry."

Grego followed Scott outside.

Scott leaned his hip against the rear fender on the pickup. Taking on a fatherly tone he said. "You know you fucked up yesterday don'cha? What do ya think I should do about it? Huh?

"I've been thinking about that Scott." Grego began. "I don't believe that it was my fault. With all those curves, the ambulance was in a blind spot when I pulled over to dump the guy. It was perfect, a nice wide spot, steep hill, everything you asked me to look for. Things just worked out badly that's all."

"Well! It may not be your fault, but *you* did — do the job. It didn't turn out too good. Now it's up to *you* to do something to fix it." Scott said opening the car door. Without warning he caught Grego's wrist and slammed the door closed on two of Grego's fingers.

Grego was so stunned and the pain was so strong that he was unable to make a sound. He looked at Scott's face and was terrorized by what he saw. He passed out with his hand still closed in the door.

Scott saw the little man start to fall. He opened the door, and lowered him to the ground with the wrist he still had hold of. He felt the wrist bones click and pop as he tried to keep him from falling.

When he saw his friend go to the ground, Tuc was out the door faster than he had moved in a long time. "What happened?" He roared as he neared the truck, his eyes bulging out in astonishment. He knelt down and picked up the little man. — He glared at the man inside of Scott's eyes. He didn't know the man he was looking at. The evil he saw made him hold his tongue silent.

Grego was just coming out of his faint. Two of his of his fingers were broken. He screamed and clutched his hand to his chest.

Tuc carried his friend into the house, set him on the kitchen counter and gently lifted Grego's hand to the faucet. He ran cool water over it and washed the blood away. Two of the fingers were obviously broken. Both bent at the same odd angle. He asked Rosco to get him a towel, and was there any ice left in the cooler?

Scott handed a piece of paper to Rosco and said, "That's the name of the town that the ambulance was from." Take him to this Farewell, Oregon place and get his hand fixed. Grego, tell them you need charity because you're transitory and have no money. Tell him you were beggin' money and got their car door slammed on your fingers as payment. Rosco you can be the good Samaritan that brought him to the hospital. While you're there Grego, you can ask a lot of questions like you're the type that talks a lot 'cause you're in pain or just nervous. Like, — 'Get many people in tonight? 'Wouldn't wan'ta take up your time if you have somebody important to take care of. Any bad accidents lately?" Scott recited. "You need to find out if that guy is there. Was he hurt bad? Did anybody die? Find out whatever you can before you leave."

"What if he is there, what then?" Tuc asked.

"Then they bring that news back here to us." He glowered at Tuc and then backed off from what he saw in the big man's face.

"Get going' now, it will take a while to get there." He said portending with parental concern. "Maybe twenty miles. Want a pain pill, Grego? No! Sorry! *little smile* — maybe not — if they give you something it could over dose ya."

Grego would not look at Scott, he kept his eyes closed against the pain. He put his good arm around Tucs' shoulder as the big man picked him up, and carried him to the truck.

Tuc returned to the house to find Scott had locked himself in the bedroom. He tapped on the door but received no answer. *Probably hiding 'cause Rosco's not here,* he thought as he listened closely at the door he heard absolutely nothing. He thought that he would have heard breathing or movement. *Maybe he's holding his breath or something.* That was just fine with him, he wasn't sure what he would do to the man. As soon as Grego came back he was going to talk to him about striking out on their own. There was something very wrong with Scott. He made Tuc very uncomfortable. He was not like the guy that he knew in prison. He was another person inside Scott's body. Tuc could feel it. Tuc was unaware that Scott needed medication for *anything. And — who is this guy Sammy, I hear him talking to when he thinks he's alone or when he's sleepin?* He wondered to himself.

# ROSCO

It took close to an hour to get to the Dune Pines Hospital in Farewell, Oregon. Rosco had stopped by the store on the way to get a small six-pack cooler, a bag of ice, ready-made sandwiches, sodas and some gas and oil for the truck. He took care of the truck and pulled around to the back of the station. He poured the ice in the cooler, and put the empty bag over Grego's hand. It needed to be kept dry, the bleeding had stopped. He placed Grego's left hand, bag and all in the cooler and put some of the ice on top. "Hold the cooler on the seat next to you, it might be easier to keep your hand inside. Here," he said opening the package, "let me put one of these sandwiches in your other hand. It'll give you something else to think about. Besides we both need to eat." Rosco popped open a soda for each of them and put one of them in the cooler so that Grego could reach it.

"Why are you being so nice to me? I don't understand." Grego asks.

"I owe Scott my life, you of all people should know that. It's difficult sometimes. I can't tell the man how to live his life. I can't tell him 'don't do this or don't do that.' Now can I?"

"Yes, I know." Grego says as they pull out of the parking area and onto the road.

"He's different now that we're out. I have sworn to protect him, not to act like him or do the things he does or even cheer him on when he does something. Believe me, I don't approve of what he has done to you."

"My hand is starting to get numb in the ice. Thank you for doing this." Grego said. "It doesn't hurt as much."

"I know a lot about pain and controlling it. I've had a lot of my own. I won't talk it about though. So, don't ask." Rosco warned.

"OK Man! I know what you mean about him being different. Just before he broke my fingers. I could swear there was somebody else or something evil behind his eyes." He said with the widened eyes of someone remembering a vision of something truly evil. His voice became a graveled whisper. "It's like nothing I've ever seen in my entire life. I'm not sure if I've seen madness before but if someone were to ask me to tell them what it looks like. I'd have to tell them to look into Scott's eyes when he's upset. Why do you protect this man? He is not the same person anymore. You don't owe this crazy man a thing."

"I still owe Scott my life. If I could get this evil being out of him without hurting Scott. I could kill the evil and save Scott, then my debt would be paid."

"But you need to be a priest or something to get rid of an evil being."

Rosco tried to explain. "I don't think it's an evil *being*. It's more like an imaginary being. You know, like when something really bad, or strange, or even weird happens to someone and that it's just too much for their mind. Another personality takes over for them. The body still needs to function, like eat, sleep and so on, even if their minds can't handle what's happening —."

Grego interrupted and spoke as if he was just beginning to understand. "Damn!" He said surprising himself. "I'll bet he's bi-polar. I know what you mean. Something *really* twisted must have happened to Scott 'cause it's taking something *really* twisted to handle whatever it was. It's just not normal for anyone to act like he does. It's protecting Scott from the shock of an experience he had, like his reality isn't anchored in the here and now. His spiritual self is losing control of his physical self."

Rosco looked at Grego and wondered how much of what he was saying could be true. It made sence though. *Grego my boy. You're deeper than I thought.* "That doesn't help *us at all* right now. It's broken fingers now, but what's next. There's already three people dead. Maybe four if the biker didn't make it. Did you see the way he smiled when he told you that you couldn't have anything for the pain?"

"Haw man! I couldn't look him in the face. I believe he enjoyed that too, along *with* breaking my fingers. It scares me, the way he seems to enjoy the pain of others."

"Like he could easily cause more just to get the pleasure." Rosco added.

"I'm almost sure it was him that killed Sylvia, the way he was yankin' her head around by the hair when he was gettin' her from behind. Her neck was broken remember?"

"Yeah, you're right. I'm really sorry that happened." Rosco confessed. "I kinda liked her with all that spunk. If I hadn't taken her back to him, he would have killed me."

"Yeah! But you're bigger than he is. How could he do that?" Grego asked.

"You must understand." Rosco instructed. "I was brought up with a very strict ideology as far as religion and human behavior is concerned. My parents raised me in two religions. One, my mother was American Indian and the other, my father was Traditional Japanese. They combined what they considered the best of both and ended up agreeing on certain aspects from each, by which I was raised. It made for an unusual life style and strict standards to live by," he added and said, "The man saved my life. I am honor bound to him until I can either save *his* life or he takes *mine*. He gave my life back to me when he saved it, and he can take my life back if he thinks I have wronged him. That's the way it is. That's the way it will always be." Rosco recited.

"Damn! That's a tough way to live." Grego said in amazement. "You're very strong to stick to the rules by yourself. If it were me, and nobody was around to check up on me, the temptation to break the rules would be very strong. I don't believe I could do it alone. What's happening right now is *just not right at all.*"

"I would be dead if not for Scott's intervention. I am a person that has deep roots my faith. I am never totally alone my friend. Nobody is. First of all, God is always with us. No matter what we do in our lives he is always there. We learn from the good things, and the bad things that happen to us. They are tests. Each test we go through whether we pass or fail will give us knowledge and strength to handle whatever is next to come."

They drove in silence for a while, both deep in thought. "*We never fail at anything.*" Rosco went on to say. "Don't be the person that stands on the sidelines and says, 'I could never do that.' Or 'I wish I could do that.' A person never truly knows what they can do until they try. They either can or cannot do a thing. It is just a way of finding out what we are best suited to do. Not everybody can do everything the same way that everyone else can. We are not all doctors, book writers, pilots or athletes."

"Sold American." Grego said and put his head back against the window with his eyes closed.

"Sorry, if I'm preaching but I have very strong feelings. Even this situation that we are in now gives us a lesson that will help us in the future."

They continued along quietly for a while, then Grego broke the silence saying, "So if Tuc or I tried to kill Scott. You would kill us, and then you would be free of Scott. Is that right?"

"Yes, I would be free of Scott, but I would not have to kill you. I would just have to stop you from killing him." Rosco instructed.

They were quiet for the rest of the trip.

Grego was thinking, *I got'ta tell Tuc about this.*

Rosco spoke as they pulled into the emergency parking area. "Damn! they oughta fix this pothole. Do you want to go in alone?"

"Not really. Do you mind?"

"That's fine. I'll go in with you."

"I'm kinda nervous. Never did like doctors and I've never had to ask for charity before."

"OK. Let's go."

"I appreciate this. I'm really a chicken when it comes to pain." Grego said thankfully.

Rosco pulled his long, black, straight hair out of the ponytail at the back of his head before going around the truck to help Grego. He was allowed to keep his long hair in prison. He claimed religious privilege. The pictures of him that were taken when he was arrested all showed his hair tied back. He needed a disguise. This would have to do for now. Rosco opened the door for Grego and sort of half carried Grego into the emergency room. "You just take a chair and hold on to the cooler and keep your hand in there. I'll do the talking."

In the emergency room Rosco helped Grego to a chair, then went to talk to the nurse. Looking at her name tag, Rosco said, "Excuse me — Carmine?" With the charm that usually got him any woman he wanted. "This guy has a couple broken fingers. He was packing groceries into these people's car for pocket change. Instead of paying him, they slam the door right on his hand. They opened the door to let him get his hand out, then drove off laughing! Can you believe that? I tried to help him all I could but, it's pretty bad. I couldn't just leave him there, so I brought him over here hoping that you could help him." He showed his beautiful teeth, when he smiled. "I've got about thirty dollars if that will help." Rosco said all wide-eyed and honest like a good Samaritan. Very charming indeed and turned his head so that his hair would cascade over his shoulder as he spoke. Women loved his hair.

Carmine smiled and said, "Why don't you wait here a minute and I'll see what I can do for you. Thinking to herself with delight, *What a charming gentleman. And, he stopped to help a perfect stranger.* She went to the delivery room to find the doctor in charge. "Ahh!" She said as Dr. Handle came through the door. "There's a gentleman that brought a transient in with a couple broken fingers. Do you want to take a look at him?"

"Yes! of course. I'm in a good mood right now. I just delivered a beautiful, healthy baby girl. You know what that means." The doctor said. "I'll change and clean up first. Take him into the examination area. I'll be right there."

When Carmine Ruiz came into the waiting area, she saw that this very charming man was comforting the injured man. *How thoughtful.* She said to herself. Then aloud she said. "The doctor will see to him now. You're very lucky. The doctor is in a good mood. He just delivered a healthy, baby girl.

"How wonderful." Rosco said, as he helped Grego into the examination room. "I'll bet that's a joyous thing to witness. A brand-new human being."

Grego passed out from the pain of moving his hand. Rosco didn't let him fall to the floor, he just swooped him up in his arms. Carried him into the examining area and laid him on the table without a second thought. Natural as can be. He smiled at her again.

This truly charmed Carmine beyond words and she flushed pink in the cheeks. Besides his beautiful hair and his charm, he was tall, gentle and very strong. *Mmm! Where has this guy been all my life. I believe my knees are trembling.* Clearing her throat, she said. "Make sure he doesn't fall off the table. I'll be right back."

When she got to the other side of the curtain, she put one hand on the wall and the other spread across her heart. She stood there silently a few seconds until her knees steadied themselves. She took a deep breath, swallowed and continued on her way.

When she returned Doc Handle was right behind her.

He said. "Let's see what we have here. Mmm! Somebody did a good job here. Packing it in ice *and* keeping it dry." He said and looked at Rosco.

Grego regained consciousness and moaned with the pain.

"Easy, easy!" The doctor said and gave the nurse instructions then looked at Rosco. "This makes my job easier. Thank you. Do you have training?"

Rosco smiled shyly. "I learned a lot from my sister, she's an LVN [Licensed Vocational Nurse], and a traveling missionary."

"My mother was a nurse on the reservation where we lived as missionaries. She made sure that everyone, including my sister and I, had knowledge of basic first aid." Rosco recited, from the many times he had used this story to avoid questions about his real life.

Carmine came back with medication and the material the doctor had requested. She swabbed Grego's arm, gave him morphine for the pain and asked Rosco. "Are you going to wait around for him?

"I was going to take him to a shelter. Could you tell me where to find one?" Rosco had his youth and the combination of Indian and oriental blood. This made him look mysterious and wise — people believed whatever he said, and didn't question further. People just took everything he said as fact. That's part of why he was in jail. His mouth charmed too many ladies out of their money. That was fine until one of the ex-husbands lost his life when he challenged Rosco. Latent jealousy made him believe that Rosco was her lover. Which he was until she ran out of money. That's another story.

Doc Handle told Rosco he would have to wait outside in the lobby.

Rosco majestically bowed his head and smiled at Carmine as he backed out, to the other side of the curtained area. He went to the waiting area and read magazines.

+++++

Rosco had slouched down in his chair so comfortably as to almost be asleep. Had been so deep in thought that he was startled when he discovered Carmine touching his shoulder. He bolted to a straight sitting position. "Oh! I'm sorry! Sir! The gentleman that you brought in, is ready to leave. We have given him some pills for the pain. Codeine tablets. Would you tell the people at the shelter that the doctor wants to see him again in three days, or if the bandage gets soiled to come in before that? It must be kept clean and dry to prevent infection."

"The doctor would be here to tell you about it, but the lady that had the baby, is delivering another one right now. That makes it twins. A double blessing. Three and a half hours apart. That doesn't happen often. I believe it might make a record for this hospital. I'll have to look it up." Carmine said all bubbly and full of smiles.

"Wow I didn't realize I'd been here that long. Did you find a shelter I might take him to?"

"Something just as good."

"I really appreciate all you've done. I'm sure Gary does too."

"Who? He gave us his name as Charlie Cotton," Carmine said.

"I thought his name was Gary. My mistake! I must have misunderstood. Guess he was in a lot of pain when he tried to tell me earlier. I got'ta get going down the road. I'm headed for Canada. My sister is working with some French Indians up there, thought I'd help out some."

Carmine told Rosco that the town wasn't really big enough to have a building set aside for sheltering purposes, but there was a rooming house that was willing to take him for a couple days free of charge. Quite possibly he might stay on and work for room and board. He could rake leaves, paint porch steps, or even clean window screens. They would see what he might be able to do as his hand gets better. There was always the sheriff's daughter, Jill. She's in a wheelchair, and might need some things taken care of around her place."

Rosco interrupted her before the conversation could go on at length. He was very tired and she seemed to have a lot to say. "You know! I've been thinking. I might just stop at my cousins' place not too far from here. I could take Charlie there and bring him back to see the doctor. I'm thinking my cousin might have a permanent job for him if he wants it. After all he was begging for money when he got hurt. Right? At least he was trying to *work* for the money."

"Yes! That's very kind of you. You don't even know this guy and you're willing to alter your traveling plans to help him out. I just hope if I'm ever in trouble, I could meet a kind stranger like yourself." Carmine praised.

"Oh please! You're making me blush. I'm just treating another fellow human being like I would want to be treated, were we to trade places. Perhaps Charlie will pass my kindness along to someone else in need. Rosco said casually. "I'd better get Charlie and get moving. I'll try to talk him into going with me *after* I get him in the car. Thanks for everything. Tell the doctor congratulations on the double birth, and thanks for seeing this guy 'Charlie'."

Carmine said. "I'll go get Charlie now. If you'll bring your car around to the entrance door. I'll bring him out in a wheelchair. He's still pretty groggy with the medication we gave him. Don't let him take any codeine for at least four hours, he just had another shot of Morphine about thirty minutes ago.

"OK. I can handle that. And thanks again. I'll be right outside in a couple minutes." Rosco said as he walked out the door.

+ + + + +

Carmine helped Rosco put 'Charlie' in the pickup It seemed more comfortable for Charlie to lay down sideways on the seat, than sitting up. They drove out of the parking lot right past a sheriff's car. The officer was talking on his radio. As Rosco drove towards the exit, the patrol car cruised up behind them. That was enough to get Rosco's heart going. He placed his right hand on Grego and told him not to move until he said it was OK. The pickup stopped at the entrance to the main road and turned left. Looking in the rear-view mirror, Rosco saw the police car turn right going the other way. He let out a breath that he was unaware that he was holding. "OK you can set up anytime you like."

Grego said groggily, "What was that all about?"

"Police car was right behind us, but it turned the other way." Rosco assured Grego. They headed for Scott's place.

"Rosco?" Grego said after a short time.

"Yes? Oh! You *are* awake."

"I was just wondering what I'm going to tell Scott. They knocked me out in there, when they operated on my hand. You should see the x-rays. I have two fingers broken in five places. I also have a sprained wrist. Scott expected me to ask a lot of questions. I couldn't think of anything but the pain. What am I going to do, Rosco? I'm not sure that Scott will understand, if the *evil one* still has control of him."

"Let me think for a while. You just rest. OK?"

They rode along for a while in silence.

"Grego? You awake?"

"Yeah! This hand is starting to hurt. Mmmm! Feels like my heart is beating inside of it." Grego complained.

"You need to hold it up above your heart. Your injured fingers are a weak spot and too much blood is trying to go to that area. It's nature's way. When we get hurt the blood rushes to it. That feeling should go away in about three days." Rosco instructed.

"How do you know so much?"

"Just experience. Been there. Done that." Rosco said quickly to wave off any praise. "Listen! What I wanted to say is this." He said commanding attention. "When we get there, I'm going to carry you into the house. You're going to be knocked out." Rosco waited for agreement.

"OK! So far. I can do that. Grego said. "Let me tell you in advance 'thanks' OK?"

"Sure, but listen. I'll tell Scott that neither one of us was able to ask questions. I'll also tell him that I tried but couldn't get anyone to talk to me 'cause they had a big emergency come in and no one had time to talk. Besides, you need to go back in three days anyway. I'll tell him that we will ask our questions then. How does that sound?"

"OK! But, how do you know that he'll go for what you tell him. How do we make him sit still for three days?"

"You know? I really think that he would believe just about anything I tell him, since he saved my life. He's not really that smart. He's just a bully that gets angry to cover up his ignorance. Like his act of saving my life, made me totally honest and faithful to him. I made a promise not to tell anyone *how* he saved my life. Somehow *he* believes that fact, means I wouldn't *lie* to him either. Which is far from the truth because he *only* has the right to take my life back if he believes I have wronged him. I wouldn't hesitate one bit, to lie if it would keep him from killing me. I am not a fool. I wish very much to keep my life. Let's just leave it at that. OK?" Rosco finished.

"OK. I'll trust you on this. I believe you want to live as much as I do."

They were silent for the rest of the trip to Scott's place.

When they arrived, it was late in the evening and both Scott and Tuc were asleep in separate rooms. Rosco and Grego entered quietly. Rosco silently tried Scott's door — it was locked. He returned to the living room to sleep on the foldout couch.

Grego went to the spare room to see Tuc. The big man woke up the minute he heard the door open. He sat up on the edge of the bed, and spoke in lowered tones. "Grego! How are you my friend?" He said patting to bed next to him. Then a frown came across his face when he saw the bandages. The frown was replaced by anger. "If that bastard had not locked himself in his room when you guys left, I'm sure I could have beat him pretty well within an inch of his life. Then I would have killed —. You know there's sompthin' very, very wrong with Scott. He's kind of creepy. I saw — like he's turnin' evil — sompthin' in his eyes."

Grego sat on the edge of the bed and leaned against Tuc, who put his giant hand on the little man's shoulder. "You know what?" Grego asked.

"No. What?"

"I'm a little groggy right now. But, when we get some time to ourselves, I will explain to you, what I learned tonight. By the way Rosco's not our enemy," he yawned. "That fact gives me understanding and hope. He got up walked to the other side of the bed, laid down and fell into an immediately drug induced sleep.

Tuc laid down on his side of the bed and thought about his friend. *Damn you Scott. Damn you for hurting little Grego. You will not touch him again.* After an hour he was still so upset he couldn't sleep, so he eased out of bed and quietly left the room. In the kitchen he found some cold coffee in the pan and warmed it up. There was a half bag of chips too. He found some dip in the cooler. He sat at the table and waited for the coffee to heat up.

Rosco poked his head in the door. "Mind if I join you?" he asked softly.

Tuc motioned him in silently by sliding, lifting a chair away from the table without making any noise.

It was understood that neither one of them wanted Scott to wake up. They smiled at each other and sat quietly waiting for the coffee.

Rosco got up quietly and left the kitchen. When he returned, he closed the kitchen door behind him and set the portable TV on the table and turned it on to a low volume. He whispered. "There's still no news but I thought we might see if there is a movie on. OK?"

Tuc nodded his head and gave Rosco a big smile.

# THE WALL

Carl read the list again and afterward he sat there silently trying to remember forgotten things, places, and people — anything. He drifted back to sleep and found that he had walked right into a wall that looked to be made out of Multi-colored, pastel crystals with a smooth, flat, scale like surface. It was like Mica and very large, one crystal was as big as a manhole cover. He didn't have to pull very hard before one of the largest crystals pulled away from the wall. It came away in his hand, uncovering a large hole in the wall. He couldn't see all the way through the wall because of the wall's thickness and the curved passageway inside. It was more like a small tunnel. *Yes!* He told himself. "This is the wall I remember seeing it from up on the hill. Another way out" he said, and then asked, "Out of where? Out of where I was before or out from behind this wall." No answer came. As he crawled into the tunnel it curved and narrowed. He was within inches of the walls outer/ other side layer, and his way out. He stretched his arms out but could not come in contact with the other side. He was stopped by the shrinking size of the tunnel ahead of him, and a layer of crystals like the one he had just pulled from the other side of this wall to get in here. He needed to go back to get some tools, so he could enlarge this area and knock the scales off the other side. He needed help.

His arms were stretched over his head in an effort to reach the other side of the wall from inside. He had push himself with his legs into the narrowing tunnel and become wedged tightly. He was stuck. He kicked, twisted, tried everything he could think of, but there was no hand or foothold for him to push or pull against. "Dear God, what to do now?" It seemed like the harder he tried the tighter he became trapped and it was getting harder to breathe.

"Carl, it's Crystal, this dream has frightened you so much that you're projecting very strong thoughts. May I stay with you in this place?"

"Please do. I'm really confused and scared. I have reached an impasse. It feels like the wall has wrapped itself around my waist. It's holding me in place. I can neither go forward or backwards. Please help me." Carl pleaded.

Crystal explained. "First of all, you need to relax so you understand what it is that's happening to your body. Your brain, will make a bypass circuit through an unused area of your gray matter and when the chemical is no longer blocking your memories it will dissipate through lack of function. It draws energy and creates a bonding agent with you. You need to build a bridge *over* it, not tunnel through it. It can only remain active as long as you are in contact with it. With no function it will dissolve away. This wall you are involved with is made of crystals. The wall of crystals represents the drug you were given. You need to go *over* this wall. Going through the wall invites contact and energizes the drug and the bond gets stronger. We are not prepared to do this now. I'm going to pull back now." She placed her hand on his shoulder.

"Wait!" Carl's eyes popped open. He was perspiring and she found his blood pressure above normal. "I think, I just found something out," he said amazed.

"What's that?" Crystal looked in his direction.

"When I'm in *dream* mode. I come right out of it when someone touches me." He recounted.

"That's right and we might have to put a sign above your bed, 'DO NOT TOUCH IF SLEEPING' What do ya think? I'm serious."

"Mmm I don't know. What if— I'm having a nightmare? Like just now, I needed someone to touch me. I'll have to think about it," Carl said pondering the possibility.

"Just an offer, I'm not pushing. You need to be aware of your options that's all. Please Carl, don't ever mistake what I say for a command, or an order. Whatever I say to you is always an option. More like bits of information or an instruction that can be either followed or not. Ruby and I can never make you do something that you would never do in the first place. We are only guides, not leaders. Everything that happens will be under your sole control. My sister and I have the ability to help you through difficult areas. We can teach you, by helping you. At any time, you may stop part of, or all of a procedure for any reason, you need not say a word. *Pulling back* is simple to do and can be done without any assistance. Just remember, you are in complete control at all times."

Sitting up and sliding his feet to the floor Carl said. "I am so thankful to be here instead of somewhere else. I shiver to think of going through this without you and everyone's help. I can't help but think that I would be totally lost." Sliding his arms into the sleeves on his robe and tying the belt, Carl invited Crystal for a soda from the vending machine.

When they left the room, Steve locked the door and escorted them down the hall.

As they walked, Crystal mentioned Steve Smith, the police guard, *as her cousin but 'don't tell the FBI'.* Steve is five foot ten and one-half inches tall. He has an average build that's a little round on edges that haven't been hardened by life or maturity. His hair is white-blond like Crystals with the palest forest green eyes anyone has ever seen.

Carl said, "They probably already know."

Steve walked behind Crystal and Carl as they spoke to each other.

Crystal told Carl "Fate has a hand in everything. Some people think of fate as destiny. She explained that our future is already determined. How we get to there from here, is up to us. We can do it the hard way, all by ourselves, or an easier way with the help of friends and people around us. From the beginning man was not created to be alone. Eve was created for Adam, as a helpmate. If one cannot share labors and accomplishments then there is no true joy in doing just for yourself. Without joy what is life? Carl, you are here because there is something to learn that will strengthen you for the life that is ahead. No one can tell you what is in store for you. The people that you come in contact with along your path of life, can help or hinder your progress. Your future depends on who, you *allow* to cling to you. Nobody can do it alone and it's best to be picky about your friends and partners. Some people will be attracted to you because of the strength of your aura. You can't carry the world's problems. There is only one of you and there will always be those that you *have to* shed, because they are using *your* supply of energy. If you find someone that is good for you and they are willing. You can cling to each other long enough to get past, whatever is in the path ahead of you both. Partnerships don't *have* to be permanent either. Depending on *what* you're going through you may need to change partners in order to *survive* your own future. Longtime friends and partners need to be multi-talented and so do you. Don't be afraid to take a challenge, it's a place of learning. If someone else's fate is to die, then it's not your fault if you failed to prevent it. You are still here because no matter how hard these people tried to kill you or your spirit, fate said that it wasn't your turn."

"OK then, I'll make it official. Crystal Smith, will you please join in a partnership with me? Will you please tell Ruby that I would like her to make it a threesome?" Carl pleaded.

"Yes! Of course, she would." Ruby said from behind them. "I'm assuming that we're considering a partnership?"

Carl's whole face lit up with a smile.

Play acting, like being about five years old. Steve says, "I wanna play too, can I? Huh? Can I, Pleeeeasssse!" Which makes everyone laugh, because he is in full uniform, gun and all. It was a sight, to see him bouncing from one foot to the other.

Ruby says smiling. "That's up to Carl."

Carl puts his fingers to his chin, "Humm."

Crystal chimes in, "Steve's cool! He's one of the good guys Carl. He's helped us before, and he has his own talent too." She praised.

"Well, if you say so. I guess it'll be OK." Carl agreed.

"Oh! Goodie." Steve said patting his hands together teasingly. "But, seriously now 'Thank you, I'll do my best.' I'm fairly new at this but my two cousins here will keep me on the right track."

"And while you're here Steve, let me say something." Carl said "I need you and Captain Kennar to talk to Thomas about a pickup truck that we saw outside my window. Crystal and Ruby saw it in therapy." He looked at the twins and immediately there was an image of the truck in his mind. "Wow."

"Stop showing off Steve. This kind of thing is new to Carl." Ruby scolded.

"Sorry I was just introducing my talent. I guess it's kinda strong. I'm new at sharing it. It's just that you were all thinkin' of it at the same time." Steve said astonished. "Your combined auras were very potent."

"Before I found out about this— *this talent*. I thought I was going crazy." Steve confessed to Carl. "That was until I did it to Ruby quite by accident. That was before I learned to control it. My cousins here saved me from the nut house, by teaching me an understanding of what was happening to me. I can manipulate thought into a mental picture to explore at your leisure. I'll try to control it. I was just a little excited about being included. I would like to try again when I'm not on duty. That is if you don't mind, Carl." Steve pleaded.

"Until I know you a little better, I'd like one of the twins to be there." Carl said trying not to hurt the younger man's feelings.

"That's fine with me. I'll take care of the pickup truck information. Before I do anything, I'll contact the Captain." Steve said.

"In the meantime, let me say, thank you all for your kindness. I'm headed back to bed after I buy my new partners a soda." Carl said fishing a five-dollar bill into the vending machine.

To ease the tension Steve smiled and said, "Well! If you hadn't offered the soda I would have had to back out on the deal."

Everyone said, "Thanks." The twins went back to work, while Steve and Carl strolled back to the room. They nodded at the FBI, unlocked the door and entered the room. Steve said. "I'll just stand here for a minute, if that's OK. When I leave this room, each of the agents will have a soda. I'm giving them a subliminal picture of a frosty can of soda that they cannot resist. It's harmless."

About two minutes later, they heard the popping of the soda can tops. "Ha! Ha! Ha!" Carl and Steve both burst out laughing. Carl said, "That's remarkable. Thanks again, I needed that. I don't think I've had anything to laugh at in — damn I can't remember the last time I really let go and laughed out loud."

Steve said. "You're welcome. Laughter is always good medicine. In my own corny way, I try to spread as much of it around as I can."

"Well, it worked. I feel pretty good right now. Thank you." Carl said — sincerely.

Steve told him. "It was an exercise in control modification. Like starting out small. My cousins are teaching me to use my talent for good and not evil."

They stood in silence for a moment.

Steve added. "I was headed in the wrong direction with my abilities, before I learned what was happening to me. First, I had to learn that my talent is a gift and in order to receive a gift there has to be a giver. I am eternally thankful to God that I was chosen to receive this gift. I will prove that his choice was good by never using it for evil." Steve reiterated, before leaving Carl's room. "Good night. I'm right outside if you need anything or just want to talk."

"Thanks! G'night Steve." Carl said, smiling as he saw the agents, each with a soda, before Steve closed the door all the way. As he laid his head down on the pillow, he remembered a relaxation exercise that he used to do. Where this memory came from, he didn't even think about. He used the controls to flatten the bed. He took a deep breath and tightened every muscle in his body from his scalp and ears to ankles and toes. He released his tight muscles all at once and let out his breath very slowly. He continued inhaling deeply and exhaling very slowly. He was asleep by the time he let out the fourth deep breath. Zzzz. He fell to sleep without any medication tonight and slept all night.

# GREGO'S WOES

Grego awoke in the middle of the night with pain in his hand. He relieved himself, took a pain pill and went back to bed. He fell asleep with his hand off the edge of the bed. It was hanging down towards the floor which made the bleeding continue.

About an hour later the pain pill was unable to relieve the pain and the bandage was full of blood. He sat up on the edge of the bed and pushed gently on Tuc's shoulder. "Tuc!" He whispered and held up his hand to the big man. "Look! Go get Rosco. He'll know what to do. Please! I need a glass of water to take a pill with. Man! This thing really hurts."

Tuc was still in his clothes from last night. He got out of bed and went to the living room to wake Rosco but he was still awake. "Grego needs your help Rosco. His hand is bleeding a lot and it hurts him. We have nothing to use for bandages."

"There's a linen closet in the hallway. Look for some old sheets that we might tear up for bandages. See if there is anything like peroxide maybe a first-aid kit somewhere," Rosco instructed Tuc and went to see Grego. "How ya doing in here?" He asked Grego, as he entered without knocking. "Looks like you sprung a leak. Let me see that." Rosco gently cut the bandage away and dropped the pieces into the wastebasket by the bed.

Tuc came in with an old sheet, a small first-aid kit and a bottle of peroxide. "Here's the stuff you need. There's tape in the kit."

Rosco thanked him, and went to work on Grego's hand.

Tuc had not seen the injury since they returned from the hospital, until this very minute. His hand was black, bruised and swollen so much that the stitches appeared to be very deep in the flesh. "Good God! That bastard just about cut your fingers off Grego. I'd kill him if I didn't have to go through Rosco here. He didn't have to do all that, just to get you into the hospital to find out information. That's way above necessary! This really pisses now! He is nothing more than an animal that needs to be put down, before he does any more damage." Tuc was infuriated and paced the room restlessly. He couldn't keep his eyes from watering as Rosco cleaned and redressed Grego's hand.

Rosco said. "This is only temporary. In the morning I'll redress it again. I didn't know the extent of the damage myself until I saw it just now. That is *not* be messed with. You could lose one or both of your fingers. Hold your hand above your shoulder, that will take some of the pressure off of it. Our biggest concern is to stop the bleeding. You may have damage that needs to be re-stitched or cauterized but I'm not prepared to do that. I'll take you back to the hospital tomorrow if this doesn't look any better. You may need the doctor again.

"The doctor said that I should have gotten a license number. I could sue. 'This is a cruel thing to do to someone else. He couldn't imagine that someone would have an excuse that could justify doing this.' It was very upsetting to him too." Grego told Tuc and Rosco. "Those pills are pretty good. The pain seems like — Mmmm! Not as strong as before. Thanks, Rosco, I am grateful. I would have been in a lot more pain without you."

"When Rosco is finished you should lay down again, and try to sleep. You shouldn't take any more pills yet. I just counted these," he said holding up the pill bottle. "There is one missing. You must have already taken it. A person can kill themselfs by takin' too much codeine." Tuc warned with parental concern.

"He's right Grego. I'm finished. Let's try to get some rest now, for tomorrow promises to be a busy day. We will have to either sell some of the drugs or make another loan. We're running out of money. I know that we all want to keep on eating."

"Let's all hit the sack and quiet please! Let's not wake the animal." Tuc said, between his teeth before helping Grego put his feet back under the covers. "Come on little friend I'll help you settle back into bed. It's already past midnight."

+++++

About seven thirty that morning, Tuc left the bedroom quietly so that Grego could sleep. *Poor little guy had a rough night.* There was hot coffee and warm 'heat and serve' cinnamon rolls that had just been lifted out of the oven. Scott was spreading the icing on the top. He was wearing his grand-pa's B.B.Q. apron. It had been printed to look like the wearer had a tuxedo on. He had driven the pickup to the little mom and pop grocery store called "Palmer's Catch-all" about nineteen miles down the road in Wide Creek, Oregon. When he left the store, he had all the supplies they would need for at least two weeks. And, all the money the old couple had made this week. Today was bank day, and they had almost a thousand dollars already packed and bagged for the Brinks truck that was due for pick up at ten this morning. Neither Grand-ma or Grand-pa would be tellin' anybody who took the missing items or the money. They each had been injected with air bubbles directly into their hearts. Air is good, Scott had told himself, "You can't trace air like you can a bullet or a drug." He was sure that the authorities knew about the drugs by now. *Maybe, well hopefully, I can sell some of the drugs.* He thought.

"Good Morning, everybody." Scott said cheerfully. "I hope you slept well; I know I did." He said settling into the chair at the head of the table. "When you get some coffee down, there's more groceries in the pickup. Some of it is frozen and, in the coolers, I picked up but we need to get it in out of the sun. Rosco, please get the tarp out of the garage, and cover the pickup when it's empty, will ya? You did park it in the back yard didn't cha?"

Rosco spoke, almost choking on a mouth full of pastry. He managed to keep his cool and swallowed it down with coffee and did a good job of covering his surprise. "You drove it last Scott, and yes—" He exaggerated the effort to look out the kitchen window. "It *is* in the back yard.'

"Thanks for heating up these rolls and makin' the coffee by the way. That's very thoughtful of you Scott. — Come on Rosco. The truck's settin' in the sun. Let's get the other stuff before it thaws out." Tuc said on his way out the back door.

When they reached the back yard, Tuc turned to look in the direction of the kitchen door and said, "Is he losin' it, or is he on some kind of high?"

They both shrugged and turned to the job at hand. They brought the groceries into the house and Scott started putting things away. There were seven coolers full of ice, TV Dinners, cold beer and sodas in the back of the truck. There must have been at least twenty plastic groceries bags full of shelf items. By the time the last bags were brought in, Scott had disappeared.

"Noooo!" Grego screamed from the spare room.

For a man of his size, he moved very swiftly. Tuc was down the hall and into the spare room before Grego's first scream fell silent. Tuc burst through the door to find Scott tugging on Grego's bandages.

"Leave it alone. Pleeeeeease! It hurts!" Grego screamed.

Tuc grabbed Scott from behind and hurled him off of the bed into the mirrored closet door. The glass cracked but did not break, Scott stayed where he was on the floor. Tuc whirled around to see Rosco coming into the room. He held up his hands, palms facing Rosco. "My fight is not with you; I am protecting my friend.

Rosco slowed his entrance, and went to check on Scott. He seemed fine. Rosco turned to see about Grego who was rolling back and forth, crying with pain. There was fresh blood on the bandage, which was hanging, half torn off his hand.

"Let me see that Grego." Rosco said, and gently held the hand in his. "Why did he do this? This doesn't make sense."

Grego was still crying with the pain.

Tuc could stand it no more. He walked over to Scott's unconscious body. He gathered Scott's shirtfront into a ball with one hand. He pulled the body off the floor, with one hand and raised his other hand up into a striking fist. Tuc said, "Rosco, this animal needs killing and I'm just the one to do it." Looking directly at Rosco he said, "Rosco I'm going to kill him— right now."

"No Tuc, don't do that. I'll have to stop you. Put Scott down." Rosco instructed.

To Rosco's surprise, Tuc let go and Scott fell to the floor. Still looking directly at Rosco, eyes never wavering, Tuc said. "Your debt to Scott has been paid in full my friend, for I would have killed him if you had not stopped me.

"BRAVO! My friends." Grego said and then his tears of pain were mixed with tears of joy. He laugh-cried loudly, rolling and rocking back and forth on the bed, until the pain demanded his attention.

Scott stirred and groaned on the floor, he sat up and grabbed his shoulder in pain. "Rosco get that bastard, he's not to touch me again. You are still pledged to protect me."

"Sorry! No can do. I have already saved your life, or you would not be waking up right now." Rosco smiled at Scott. "From now on I am not pledged to anyone but myself and it's about time. From now on, you'll have to behave yourself or pay the consequences like anyone of us is expected to do. Nobody here is better than the other. We are all in this together do you understand?"

"Well! If you're going to be that way about it. I guess I have no choice. You say that you have saved my life and I have no reason to disbelieve you." Scott smiled and headed for the kitchen. "Now let's get something to eat, I'm starved," said Scott, grabbing his shoulder in pain."

Looking at Tuc, Rosco asked "Would you mind getting the first-aid kit and the other stuff we had last night? Please I need to redress Grego's hand."

"Sure Rosco." When Tuc returned with the things Rosco needed he said. "You think we can trust Scott? He's got all those drugs. I'm not going to eat anything that I didn't unwrap myself. I volunteer to fix everyone else's food if necessary.

"How are you feeling Grego? What was he doing to your hand?"

"He said he wanted to see how bad my hand was. So, he grabbed my wrist, *my sprained wrist*, and started to pull the Band-Aids off. He was grinning. He wanted it to hurt. I know he did." Grego explained while his hand was being fixed *again*. They gave him another pain pill. He drifted into a restless sleep, and slept until about eleven a.m. the next morning.

+ + + + +

Each time Rosco and Tuc checked on Grego during the night there was more blood on his bandages. They were both becoming concerned because of the bleeding and Grego didn't look too good either. The uninjured fingernails on his injured hand were beginning to look blue. They left him to sleep.

+ + + + +

Tuc said to Rosco. "I'm hungry. What about you?"

Yeah! Come to think about it I could use something to eat right about now. Let's go see what's for brunch.

Scott was supplicating pleasantly when they came in the kitchen. "Can I fix you guys something to eat?"

"Nah! I'll get it." Tuc said rummaging through the stuff Scott hadn't put away yet. "You guys want a cold beer?"

Scott and Rosco each accepted a beer. I'm going to put a couple TV dinners in the oven. What kind do ya want?

"Whatever's on top" Rosco said.

"I'll take a 'fried chicken' one." Scott said popping the top open on his beer can and drinking down about half of it in one guzzling swig. Then set the can down heavily (*manly to Scott's way of thinking*) on the table. Some of the liquid splashed on his hand and he licked it off with a smug smile.

While Tuc heated up the dinners, Scott pulled a wad of money out of the bag that he had on the floor by the table. "Here! We share equal, right?" He said, while he made four piles of money. When he finished there was one hundred and seventy dollars in each pile. He didn't tell them about the three hundred that he'd pulled out and stashed in his bedroom, before bringing the bag into the kitchen.

Tuc reached over and took two piles, saying that he would see to it that Grego got his.

Scott picked up his stack of bills, took two twenties and put them in his shirt pocket. He handed the rest of his share to Tuc, and said "Here give this to Grego for his pain and suffering. I feel really bad about his hand. I don't know what came over me to do a thing like that. Sometimes

I'm just not myself. The medication that I was taking in the joint, kept me from the *bad feelings* like I get sometimes." Scott confessed, hoping for sympathy. It had worked before; he might as well try again. These guys were pissed at him, he could tell. Sammy always got him in trouble. If only Sammy would stay away a little while longer. Things would be OK again.

Rosco pulled the TV out of his jacket pocket, and set it on the table. Still unable to get news, or anything about *them*. There was a story about an older couple that owned and operated a small food and supply store in Wide Creek, Oregon called "Palmer's Catch-All." A customer who called the police department found them on the floor. Apparently, there was no struggle. The customer said that 'there was a whole bunch of groceries missing'. He could tell 'cause the owners always kept the shelves and frozen food areas full. They did a pretty good business here. People come from all over the place, 'cause they know they can find what they need.

The news reporter from the television station was doing a live interview and held her microphone in front of the Brinks truck driver. He said. "I was scheduled to pick up a bank deposit today." Pulling the microphone away from the driver, the reporter said. "The dollar amount won't be known until it is confirmed from the paper work that was sealed in an evidence bag, that will be gone over by the local police department. And how much did they get away with?" The Brinks driver said. "I usually picked up around eight hundred to a thousand dollars every week. This little store does a pretty good business. They carry a lot of specialty items and custom orders." He smiled at the camera as the reporter's voice identified herself, the station and promised to be back with more details as they came in.

Rosco turned the portable TV off. Tuc and he looked at each other.

Scott said with hidden relief, "Sounds like he's trying to be more important than he is. You guys saw how much there was right here on the table."

Tuc and Rosco looked at Scott with surprise. Rosco said, "You did this? — So that's where all this stuff came from. I was thinking that you sold some of those drugs we picked up earlier."

"Nah!" Scott said "That stuff's too hot right now. Besides, we don't have any connections here that we can *off load* to.

"So how did you off the old folks?" Tuc asked.

Scott smiled inwardly at the memory and then moved the smile to his face. "The old lady fainted when she saw me grab her old man from behind and pump a syringe full of air into his heart. I just did her right where she was layin'. No fuss no muss. I think she'd already had a heart attack. I picked up the moneybag from the office and went shopping. They had coolers on sale and a freezer full of ice. That's when I got the idea about how to get all this stuff home without it melting. There's ice cream in one of the coolers, too. It was kinda neat having the whole store to myself. You see! They hadn't opened up for business yet. Only the back door was unlocked. I locked it behind me as I went in and scolded them like a concerned son about how dangerous it was to be so careless. Then I showed them what could happen to them —" Scott sat there smiling at the memory, and said no more.

"Here's your dinner" Tuc said sliding it over to Rosco.

Rosco said, "Thanks" and walked into the living room with the TV and the dinner. "Thanks for the money Scott." He said, from the doorway.

Tuc told Scott. "Thanks for the money." He picked up his dinner and headed for the next room with Rosco. Before he left the kitchen, he told Scott. "Your dinner will be done in about ten minutes; the chicken takes longer. Please be sure to turn the oven off when you're through. OK?"

"Yeah fine! Thanks for cookin' it for me."

"You're welcome." Tuc said and disappeared around the corner, stopping any further conversation.

+++++

After he finished eating, Rosco went to check on Grego. He immediately turned around and went to get Tuc. They both rushed back to the bedroom. Grego was sitting on the edge of the bed, holding his injured hand up in the air above his shoulder. The bandage was almost completely red. The bleeding had not stopped.

"Why didn't you call somebody?" Rosco asked and told Tuc about the small cooler that he had used before. It was on the back porch. Would he please put some ice in it and bring here with a trash bag?

Tuc brought the small cooler into the kitchen and started to fill it with ice from one of the big coolers. Scott asked what he was doing. Tuc answered him through his teeth letting Scott know not to mess with him. "The hand that you broke has not stopped bleeding. It needs to be packed in ice."

Tuc finished and headed for the spare room. Walking to the door, he paused and looked at the man he wanted to kill. He squinted his eyes, and still speaking through his clinched teeth, said. "He probably needs to go *back* to the hospital. No thanks to you."

"Sorry! I just didn't believe that it was that bad." Scott pleaded

"If you didn't believe it then why didn't you just *cut* the bandage off to look at it?" Rosco asked from the doorway.

"I don't know I guess I thought that it would pull right off." Scott answered. Thinking— *Oh! Man! Sammy, I don't need this big guy pissed off at me. Let's keep it down for a while. OK?*

Rosco had come to the kitchen to see what was taking so long to get the ice. Rosco took the cooler to the sink and added water. He opened the trash bag and stretched it over the cooler so that Grego could put his hand down into the ice water without getting his hand wet. "Hurry up now Tuc, make sure that his hand is inside the bag like this." Rosco demonstrated with his own hand inside the bag and pressing his fist down into the iced water. He pulled his dry hand out of the ice and showed it to Tuc. He said, "It's very, very important that his hand is kept dry. That will keep the bleeding down."

Scott followed them back to the spare room and Grego. While Rosco redressed the damaged hand, Scott just sat there on the other side of the large bed and stared. The hand was swollen and black with bruising. The fingers were swollen so much that the stitches threatened to cut the flesh. Scott said with tears in his eyes. "Ohh! Grego, I'm sooo sorry!"

Grego replied. "Yeah sure! Easy for you to say."

"Honest! I had no idea that it would turn out like this." I was only wanting an excuse, a *little* excuse, to get you inside the hospital.

Scott held out his hand to show the scars across three of his own fingers. "My grand-pa closed my fingers in that very same door one time but my fingers were only bruised and the skin was cut some. I was only fifteen years old." Scott said standing up. "Nothing like what happened to you with broken bones. That looks pretty bad. I thought I would have to shut the door harder 'cause grown up fingers are bigger. I'm taking you back to the hospital as soon as Rosco here, gets through fixin' you up."

Grego said. "That's OK Scott. Rosco can take me. He knows right where it's at. I was in too much pain to remember how to get there. I couldn't tell you the directions." Grego said to Scott and pleaded with his eyes to Rosco. *'You take me. Please???'*

"I can take him, Scott it's no problem. I really don't mind." Rosco pleaded, being very casual with his tone of voice.

"No! I'll take him. After this morning's little drive. I discovered that I like driving grand-pa's old truck. I need to get out in the open air. This house is becoming like a prison. I've got 'Cabin-Fever' so to say." Scott said with a smile.

Rosco and Tuc could do nothing but look at Grego with *'I'm sorry'* in their eyes.

When Scott left the room, Rosco said. "What can we do? It's his truck."

"I know and if it weren't for the pain, I would have gone with him. I need help with this thing. It really hurts a lot. Besides he seemed to be truly sorry. I think the tears were real." Grego said hopefully with a flicker of doubt in the back of his mind.

"If he hurts you again, I will kill him the next time I get my hands on him. I'm going to find him right now, and tell him." Tuc said and left the room.

He found Scott in the kitchen making a couple sandwiches for the trip. "I want to make it clear to you right now." Tuc raised his voice, "*DO NOT* harm Grego anymore than you already have. I had the opportunity to kill you earlier today, but I told Rosco that I would not and I did not. If, Grego tells me that you even looked at him wrong, I will settle it for my helpless and injured friend. Don't think for one minute that I would stop, the next time I get my hands on you. Remember this. If you hurt Grego. You hurt me. So, don't touch him." Tuc said towering over Scott.

"Easy! Easy! Down big fella." Scott had his hands out in front of him, palms facing Tuc. "I understand big guy. This is not going to be a problem. I promise! I'm so truly sorry about his hand. I *promise* that I will do nothing to make his injury any worse.

With his voice lowered, only slightly. Tuc said, "His injury or any other part of him and remember my warning. I *can* do what I say, if you *provoke* me. — Make an extra sandwich for Grego, he hasn't eaten since you hurt his hand. He shouldn't take those pain pills on an empty stomach. They'll make him sick. A couple soda's too." He said and walked out of the kitchen. He headed for the spare room.

Grego was sitting on the edge of the bed with his hand inside of the bag that kept it dry. It was submerged in the cooler. Grego was in a lot of pain at the moment. Rosco was telling him. "I know, it hurts really bad when you first put it in the ice. The pain will go away, as soon as the ice can make your hand cold enough. It will be nice and cold, and the cold will help the swelling go down. I promise, just hold it there another minute, you'll see."

Grego said "I'm going to need help Mmmm! getting to the truck."

Tuc said "We'll just put the cooler on your lap and I'll carry you outside."

Rosco said, "There are a few things we need to talk to each other about, but Scott needs to hear this too.

Scott stuck his head in the door. "Is Grego ready?"

"Yes, but come here first. You need to hear this." Scott came in and sat on the edge of the bed again. Rosco continued, "When we went to the hospital before, Grego's name was Charlie Cotton. The story was, that he was helping put groceries in a car for spare change. These people paid him by shutting his hand in their car door. I as a witness and good Samaritan, after trying to help him and discovering that it was broken, brought Charlie here to the hospital. I offered them thirty dollars but they didn't take it. The doctor treated him for free because he was in a good mood. He had just delivered a baby and it was his custom to treat the next patient for free. I believe they only said that because we asked for charity. They didn't want to make us feel bad for having no money. The people there, they treated us real nice. The emergency room nurse, her name is Carmine Ruiz. She was very helpful. She was smilin' and everything, like I was a hero for helping out this poor guy Charlie here. I believe that I charmed her with my hair. Some women just love this stuff and a story about going to Canada." He thought a moment. "Oh! yeah! To help my missionary sister out with some French Indians up there. Scott! You will have to be my cousin. You have some property out of town. I didn't give them a name or location. I took Charlie to you, my cousins. *That's your place.* So that he wouldn't have to go to a shelter.

There is a good chance that Charlie could go to work for you after his hand heals up. You could always use some extra help around the place. I didn't tell them what kind of place you have. That's up to you if Carmine should ask. Maybe Charlie tried helping out too early at your place. That's why his hand is acting up. They will be able to tell that we tried to redress the hand, because of the old sheets we have wrapped around Charlie's hand."

"OK! You ready for a ride little friend?" Tuc asked Grego as he scooped him up off the bed like a stuffed animal. Grego looks so fragile, with his small frame of five foot seven inches being carried by, Tuc's Weight-lifter's muscled arms and large frame of six foot four inches.

Sammy took a mental picture of the two men together. *'No! He didn't want to tangle with this big guy.'* He would think about this image if he started feeling angry again. Scott would take Charlie to the hospital peacefully.

While Tuc was helping Grego get into the truck, Rosco was showing Scott how to find the hospital, using the map.

Rosco said, "Please, both of you. Don't take everything that has happened and turn it around and make it something to be angry about. Let's have a group meeting when you guys get back. OK?" When Scott wasn't looking at him, Rosco gave Grego and Tuc a very slight nod, and they gave it back. "We need to talk about what we all want to do about *staying* out of jail. Who wants to do what? Are we going to stay together? Go our separate ways. Whatever it is. We need a plan. We can all think on it 'til you get back."

Scott tooted his horn all friendly like as they pulled out of the driveway. Rosco said, "What else could we do? Tell Scott 'no' you can't drive your own truck? *We* can't do diddley 'cause we have no transportation of our own." That worried both of them. They walked silently back through the kitchen door.

When they got back in the house, Tuc said, "Maybe we could pool our money and get a little clunker. That's what I used to do. Spend a couple— two or three hundred dollars on some old rattle trap that nobody would even remember seeing. Drive it till it broke down and got another one." Tuc reminisced with a smile. "I really don't like not having any wheels. I'm starting to feel trapped here. The way Scott's acting, he just might do something stupid and somebody will remember seeing the pickup truck. How could anyone forget a Classic like that. It's beautiful, all turquoise and white. A real eye catcher for sure.

+++++

The trip was rather quiet 'cause they were both eatin' sandwiches, and drinkin' sodas. Although he wasn't feeling well, his hand wasn't hurting much packed in the ice like that. Grego was starving and dehydrated. In the forty minutes that it took to get to the hospital, Grego had managed, single handedly to eat, two sandwiches and drink three sodas. They had an unofficial belching contest and ended up laughing, which was good for both of them. It took some stress off.

Scott became serious when they pulled into the parking area for emergencies. He told Grego. "Go on in by yourself. After they finish with you, walk on up one of the halls and come out the side doors. See there? "Scott said pointing to a door at the side of the building. Look around and in some of the rooms. Maybe you'll spot Carl. Don't try to talk to him, just see where he is in there and come out and tell me.

+++++

Doc Handle slides the curtain back, and finds Grego with his hand soaking in a brown disinfectant solution. The nurse had undressed his hand and cleaned it up so that the doctor could go to work on it right away. "Mmm! What have you been doing young man? Looks like you've been doing just about everything and pretending that you didn't have an injured hand. Am I right?"

"Well! I haven't been doing very much." Grego said with tears welling in his eyes. "Doctor this hurts so bad." The tears ran down his face as he closed his eyes against the pain and opened them again. "It started bleeding and the bandage needed to be changed. They didn't have any so they tore up an old sheet and re-wrapped it. It wouldn't stop bleeding. They changed it about three times.

"Well now! Take it easy son. These things sometimes happen. The good Samaritan does more harm than good. Old sheets and rags are fine as long as they haven't been laying around too long in the cupboard." He said as he went to work on Grego's hand. "You tell this good Samaritan that next time they decide to use old sheets or rags that it's OK, as long as they don't smell musty or moldy. You have an infection starting here. More than likely from a mold by the looks of it.

"Is it bad?" Grego asked as he winced with the pain of the doctor's probing.

"No. Not too bad. The infection is on the outside, that is much better than on the inside. Good news is that you're going to live, and have two good hands. The bad news is that it might take a while. I'm going to have the nurse pack you up a first aid kit."

"Thanks a lot doctor. That means a lot to me. You are so kind to help me out. Is there any, *way* that I can repay you? Please! After my hand heals let me come back and return the favor. I am good with my hands and I am an artist when it comes to wood. I am a carver. You will see! It will be good therapy, I'm sure.

"Well, only if you insist. If you show up, it will be a delight. If you do not, then so be it. But either way, you owe me nothing. Did you know that there were twins the other night? The second child born that night covers this time." Doc Handle said.

"Then you were serious about that, then. I thought you were just — being charitable." Grego said with amazement.

"Totally serious, young man!"

+++++

A short time later:

"There now. I have cleaned them and replaced a couple stitches. You should be just fine. The stitches will dissolve on their own."

Carmine told him to stay on the table until she got a wheelchair.

"Carmine will be taking you to our body shop when she gets back. I'm going to have the technician fit you with a removable cast at least up to your elbow. Your wrist is still sprained. It can be removed for showers in about two weeks and you can start going without it while you're sleeping in about three weeks. Then you work your way up to not wearing it at all. Don't overdo it though, you could prolong the healing by not waiting before you put those fingers to work. I recommend you put new gauze dressing next to your skin before putting the cast back on. The skin could get infected if the gauze is not clean." Doc instructed.

"Again Doctor. Thank you for your kindness. Twins, huh?"

"Yeah! That's what I said. Amazing the feeling one gets from a single birth but with twins it's like a *BONUS*. Good night Charlie." He said moving on to his next patient smiling, remembering.

+++++

On his way out, Grego walked up the hall like Scott wanted him to. He was looking down hallways and into rooms. So far nothing — *What's this, guys in suits sitting on chairs by this room three-thirty-three and a cop talking with a patient.* He almost said it out loud but kept his surprise to himself. *Ohh! Damn its Carl. Play it cool.* He fumbled and dropped the first-aid kit. His foot kicked it, and it flew against the wall about three feet ahead of him.

A beautiful redheaded nurse picked it up for him, and smiled as she handed it to him. "Here you go." She purred with sympathy.

"You're so kind. Thank you!" He reflected her smile. *Grego!* He told himself. *Just act like normal. You're just a guy walking through the hall. You got a cast on your hand. You look like you belong here.* Carl smiled at him when they made eye contact. He smiled and nodded at Carl. Grego just walked right on by and out the door. He turned right and walked up the sidewalk to the pickup truck that was waiting by the curb.

Scott jumped out and opened the door for Grego then went around and got in behind the wheel. He turned sideways in the seat to look at Grego. "Well! What did they do to you?"

Grego held up his hand, showing the cast to Scott.

"Ohh! Man, I never meant this to happen. I'm truly sorry! He reached over to pat Grego's shoulder.

Grego's uninjured hand flew up his to ward off the attack that wasn't happening.

Scott jerks his hand back and realizes that the little man *was* afraid of him. "It's all right. I'm not going to hurt you. I'm sorry! I made you afraid of me. Sometimes I just can't control myself. I need to find some medicine like they were giving me in the joint. It always made me feel —mmm, not so angry. Being angry makes me tired." He said and then asked. "Did you see anything or anybody?"

"I saw plenty. There are Feds sitting in the hall by one of the rooms and COPS talking to patients." He exaggerated. "Let's get the *hell* out of here." He said with a motion of his good hand. Not knowing why, he had lied to Scott about seeing Carl. Letting him believe that there was more than one cop. Well! He hadn't lied really. He just didn't *tell* Scott that he'd seen the poor innocent guy that got entangled in one of his illusions. Grego knows how that feels and didn't want to push it off on someone else. Carl didn't seem to recognize him and didn't deserve to be put through anymore of Scott's crap. *Godspeed to Carl. Thank God he didn't die.* Grego had felt great sorrow when he laid eyes on Carl. He thought that, if he'd had strings on his heart then he could have said that someone had tugged on his heartstrings. It felt so real. There was just something about Carl that wouldn't let Grego betray him.

After all he was not guilty of the crime he was put in jail for. He was found kneeling beside the body of his girlfriend. Her ex-husband, escaped the scene after doing the dirty deed himself in a jealous rage. Drove down the street and called the cops about 'a lot screaming coming from a neighbor's house.'

They traveled mostly in silence. Both thinking their own private thoughts about cops. They were home in less time than it took to get to there.

Tuc was out of the house before the truck stopped. "You need help Grego?"

"Nah! I'm fine, but thank you. The doctor gave me a first aid kit. He said that the bandages we put on were sitting too long in the cupboard. They had mold or fungus on them. I'll be fine now. Wanna sign my cast?" He asked holding it up for Tuc to see. "Let's get inside. I'm kinda cold and I'm hungry."

"Grego!" Rosco said from the kitchen table and stood up. "You guys got back pretty fast."

"The doctor said it wasn't too bad. But he sent a message to my first aid giver. For your own information next time you use homemade bandages, make sure they don't smell musty or moldy. The one's we used had a mold on them, and it caused an infection to start. He replaced two stitches." Then he whispered. "Scott did that trying to pull the bandages off. He was 'OK' to me, not mean or anything. We need to talk and I mean not in front of Scott."

"After Scott goes to bed. For now, let's we play cards or something. This is not the time for that particular conversation. Let's just keep him in a good mood for now." Rosco conspired. "Hey! You guys." He shouted for everyone to hear. "How about some cards. Anybody interested, meet me in the kitchen." The first rule they made was, "No Gambling 'cause everybody need to keep what they had." There were plastic poker chips in the spare room.

"Yeah! I'm tired, but I'll put in for a couple games with ya! I haven't played cards in a while. Might be fun." Scott said rubbing his hands, locked his fingers together and bent them all backwards at once, popping several knuckles at the same time.

Grego shivered inwardly and sat down at the table. "No shuffling or dealing for me guys. I'll play *dealer* for a few games in a row after my hand gets better. OK?" He gave them an exaggerated smile, stretching his lips wide to show a lot of teeth, just to make his point, then closing his mouth quickly to a normal smile. "Let's play. What's the game?"

Tuc said. "How about Spades or we've got chips how about Mexican Sweat or Thirty-One?"

Rosco said, "Here's three chips each let's play Thirty-One, then Grego won't have to hold so many cards."

The evening went fairly smoothly. No fighting or arguing. In general, a pleasant conversation was bantered back and forth. They all had agreed that the group meeting could wait until morning, when everybody would have a clear mind and well rested body. 'Especially you Scott. You had to drive a lot today.'

Grego spoke of his adventure, embellishing his narrative. Walking down the hall, looking in rooms and hallways to see what he could and there were so many cops. Come to think of it, those guys sitting in the hall were probably the Feds. Maybe they had some big shot Mayor or something having a wart removed.

"Ha! Ha!"

# THE PARTNERS

Steve, Crystal, Ruby, Doc and Wayne were all in the living room at the twins' house. They were talking about Carl's circumstances. "I feel that he is in great danger," Crystal warned. It was a consensus with all of them. What to do, was the question.

"I'd like to project some of his images so that we could all be on the same wavelength." Steve proclaimed, then looked at his captain. "Sir, Carl asked me to tell you something. I think, if my cousins here will help me. I believe that I can show all of us the vehicle that has been bothering Carl. When I scanned him, this picture popped right out at me."

"That's a good idea if I'm going to help," Doc said. "I'm not as good at this as all of you. I'm sure if I know what I'm looking for it would help. This chemical they gave him was still in the experimental stages. It has very limited uses and then only with severe cases of psychotic trauma. These patients are considered a danger to themselves and those around them."

Ruby said. "OK. Is everybody ready? Crystal. Let's help Steve. We already know what it looks like."

Crystal says. "OK" and looks into Ruby's eyes to strengthen the image.

Steve focused them on the turquoise and white pickup truck parked by the back door.

The trance was broken when Wayne said, "Hey! I've seen that truck. Right outside of the hospital. OOPS! Sorry."

"WHOA!" Doc said. "What a rush. Nice truck though. I'll have to keep an eye open for it.

"That's OK Sir." Steve said. "Here's a short one I got from him when he told me to tell you." He said to Wayne. Please, everybody touch the person next to you, it makes this easier for me to start then you can let go. I'm already tired from the one I just did. Ready?" He flashed them a picture of two men sitting in a classic pickup truck. It was setting outside Carl's window and the two men appeared to be arguing. The big man reaching for the little one. And the smaller man putting his hand up to ward off what appeared to be a hit or strike.

It was Doc's turn to break the trance this time. "I fixed that man's hand. Twice. He has two broken fingers and a sprained wrist. He told us his name was Charlie. It's too bad. I liked the little man. Said he was an artist, a carver of wood. He promised that he would make it up to me for helping him out after his hand heals. I was looking forward to seeing him again too. Hummm!" He cleared his throat and added. "From what we saw, I wonder if the big guy had anything to do with his injured hand. They said it was smashed in a car door."

Wayne said "I'm going to double the guard on Carl right now. He's probably a spy trying to find out if Carl is here at the hospital. Excuse me while I use the phone. This needs to be done yesterday."

Crystal waited until Wayne was finished with the phone. Then she related what she had explained to Carl about building a bridge over the chemical wall that he had encountered while dreaming. She told them of the problems he was having when he tunneled into the wall. How his efforts were strengthening the chemical against him. How it would dissipate if ignored. After all it was a chemical used for controlling the psychologically disturbed patients. It would be eliminated through the natural processes of the body. Repeat dosages would be administrated if the patient showed signs of slipping back into his or her old problem. "It is still an experimental drug," she added. "The normal dosages for the drug are in very small amounts. Doc, didn't you say that there were large amounts of this drug found in his blood?"

Doc added what information he had. "Yes. A very large amount. We have reports from the laboratory that makes it, and the experimental facilities that are using it. There has been no testing of larger doses than 1.5 cc's injected. The amount we found in Carl's blood was nine times that much. The only blessing was that it is not toxic. It will not cause death by itself. This is authenticated only because of the massive dose that Carl received."

Ruby continued with the information that they had. "We know the head injury caused the amnesia. It is not known how or if, the chemical called PSY351 is preventing Carl's recovery of lost memory. PSY351 has never been used on anyone with a physical injury before. Any results we establish must be shared with the laboratory that has been developing and experimenting with it. They may want to send someone over here to examine our patient. Take some body fluids. Ask some questions. This can only be with Carl's permission, of course."

Wayne added. "This is not a drug that those government guys in the hall need to know about as of yet. We will transfer our information directly to the laboratory and they will use their own discretion on releasing the information they have after they have completed their experiments. Anyone that shows up to examine him will have to appear to be a social worker, like maybe finding out if he's being treated well and so forth."

Steve added. "There are people that will, if given the chance, take advantage of persons with unfortunate circumstances. Does he have a place to stay after he gets out of here?" He paused and said. "He could stay at my place for a while. He seems likable enough."

Still thinking along the lines of who they could say was to interview Carl, Wayne added. "Possibly a representative from his insurance company. Making sure he's not going to sue for permanent loss of memory. We'll think of something. We need to tiptoe around these Feds for now they're getting really antsy," he said and added that he would keep two police officers, or bodyguards on duty twenty-four seven.

Crystal politely cleared her throat. "Ruby and I still need to have at least one or maybe two more therapy sessions with Carl. I'm finding that he is quite receptive and has a natural *talent* of his own. I believe that his projections are read so easily by Ruby and myself because of the fact that Carl is a surviving twin."

Ruby finished sharing her thoughts with the group. "His latent talent is very close to the surface. He doesn't know that he has it yet. His twin sister Rose and he were just starting to explore their twin-factor when they were separated by an unfortunate accident. He is aware of a talent but his mind leans towards thinking that it is caused by his accident. His talent is real. His projections are so strong they nearly leap out at you. Doc do you remember saying that there was something about him that made you like him? You didn't know what it was?"

"Yes, I still feel that way."

"Well, here it is. You're sensitive to people like that. You liked the little man Charlie, with the broken fingers, too. Perhaps he's not a bad guy after all. You're more like a *sensitive* than a *psychic*. You feel the vibrations around you. Always trust what you feel. Pay attention to that funny feeling you get every once in a while. Learn to trust your feelings more than you do now. The feelings that you get from the birth of a child should tell you something about how to recognize what it feels like. You know, that feeling you get that makes you treat the next patient for free? Well, that's part of it." Crystal instructed.

"Well, I'll be jiggered", Lloyd said. "I've had those kind feelings all my life. It's nice to know I can speak of it, after so many years of holding it back. I never spoke of it in medical school. They would have locked me up for being a madman or maybe study me in a lab. It also scares the pajeepers out 'a me and then there are times I get the feeling that something is wrong. It makes my heart skip a beat like saying *'pay attention'*. It keeps me from doing certain things and later I find out that whatever it was would have either made me ill or injured me." He said, staring off into his thoughts, thinking until Steve spoke.

Anxious to leave Steve said with enthusiasm. "So! When's a good time to get together? I'm looking forward to getting started."

"Maybe in the morning. Early. Right after Carl wakes up would be an excellent time. He's more receptive at that time of day, everyone is. Let's see what Ruby and I can do tonight." Crystal said thoughtfully. "We'll tell him about our plan so that he can mentally prepare. I know Ruby and I feel an urgency to get this matter settled. The feds are not going to set on their hands much longer."

"You're right about that," Doc said. "They ask me daily, when I think he'll be getting better. They hint that they have technology that might help bring his memory back, if they could just take him to their facilities. I'm not a fool. There they can relentlessly grill, test and probe him about the drug he has in him. Where they came from and how did he get them? Nice and helpful those fed guys. Don't you think?" Doc adds. "Oh! Yeah! They said that we shouldn't have to take on the burden of helping Carl. Whatever that means. I told them that it was no burden to us, because we were being paid very well by the insurance company. Ha! Ha! That put a wrinkle in their plans to woo him away from us, with all their technology and expertise."

"I got'ta get ready for work." Steve said looking at Wayne his boss and smiling. "I wouldn't want to be late."

"That's right son. Don't be late." Wayne said with a mock frown and thumbed him to the door. "See ya later, Steve."

Steve said "good bye" and everyone answered "bye" as he shut the door behind himself.

Everybody went their own separate ways except the twins. They had some preparing to do before morning. First of all, they too had to get ready for work. They both felt that there was some kind of danger ahead. Seeing into the future, they did not do as say a fortuneteller might do. The twins were what you might call psychic guides. They needed to be with you at the time they help you. There is no helping from a distance. They couldn't tell you about far into the future, but they could guide you through anything that was in your immediate future and be with you. That is, they can help you with the 'things of the now that touch your future' or you might say 'things of the future that are connected to now.' They felt a connection with Carl the minute they first saw him. They knew that he was in trouble, that's why they left him the notebook. They offered to help him open some of the doors that had been closed to him.

# GROUP MEETING

After Scott went to bed, Grego told them about seeing Carl at the hospital. Also, the fact that Carl did not recognize Grego. "I was this close to him" He said holding up his good hand showing about eighteen inches between his fingers and his own face. The three of them decided that Carl was just an innocent victim and to leave him alone. Especially with all those cops around and the fact that he did not recognize Grego. He also told them, about his promise to the doctor. He wanted to keep his promise. The doctor is such a good person. "I don't want anything to hurt him. He reminds me of my father. God rest his soul." He felt like talking and nobody seemed bored, so he continued. Maybe it was the painkillers that had loosened his tongue. He didn't care as long as nobody complained. It felt good to say the things that he'd kept to himself for so long.

"My mother died in childbirth," he continued. "She gave me her talent. I have seen the art that she created before I was born. I never did get to tell my Dad how much I loved him. We had an argument the last time I saw him. He told me that I would waste my life away trying to be an artist. The only thing I had from my mother was her talent, and skill. I love to carve things out of wood, but in jail no knives or anything sharp were allowed. There was no money in it, my dad would say. How was

I supposed to support a family? Give him Grandchildren. No woman would want a man that had no job." Grego had stormed out the door and left his father in tears.

During the first year that he was gone away from home Grego had been arrested and convicted of murdering his girlfriend. He did not commit the crime. Her ex-husband had threatened her many times. *'He was jealous. Nobody could have her if he couldn't.'* Grego, had come home to find her on the floor. He was kneeling next to her body when the police came in.

His father had takin' ill after he had been in jail two years. He died of a heart attack. Which had left Grego alone. There was a short silence, while they all did some thinking.

Everyone had agreed that, Scott was not to know about Carl or he would be pissing and moaning about — 'We should bust in there and kill everybody including the cops.' It was decided before they went to bed. There was just something about Carl. Nobody but Scott wanted to hurt him any more than they already had. In fact, it was Scott that always caused most of the physical damage wherever they went or whatever they did. The guy is always settin' on the edge of doing something radical. The longer they stayed around him the more uncomfortable they felt. Besides the fact that he's a *control freak*. He didn't give this many orders when they were in jail.

+++++

The evening had gone well and it was now morning. It was time for the group meeting. To stop any arguments before they started, Rosco had given everybody pencil and paper. Everything would be written down. Each person was to write down things that they have been wondering about. It was to be questions about the four of them and what they were going to do. Rosco would collect all questions and then see if anybody had the same questions. He would make a list of the questions most asked first. Then have everybody write down what they thought should be the answer.

First, was on *everyone's* list. "What is next?"

Second, was on three lists "Are we going to stay a group or split up."

Third, was on two lists "We need a different car."

Rosco started the procedure. "Now, I'm going to read the questions one at a time. Each of you will write down what you think should be done to solve the problem. You can write whatever you like. Nobody can tell you that you are wrong. Everybody had the same thing on their list: 'What is next?' Write down your answers—." And, so the meeting went. One question at a time and lots of talking after everything was finished. Everyone was happy and excited about getting everything settled. The final decisions were as follows. The group would stay together until the weekend, which was two days away. By then Tuc and Grego would be able to get a car by pooling their money, and still have some leftover for gas and such. Rosco would go off on his own. He would have no trouble finding a lady. Perhaps Tuc and Grego could drop him off in a city somewhere. Scott already had a place to live, so he would stay put. The food supplies would be split up evenly. Each would take a couple of the coolers. It was decided to have a little party this weekend to celebrate their new found independence.

Sammy and Scott were happy to finally have the whole house to themselves. *Freedom in just two days.* Scott was a little unsettled at living alone and having to take care of Sammy, but he loved Sammy and would always take care of him. After everyone left, they would have to talk about sharing the chores around here. Sammy told Scott that he didn't mind at all, taking over some of the responsibilities around here. After all he loved Scott. Didn't he?

# REPORTS

**W**hen Wayne got to work, there was a stack of paperwork waiting. Approval forms, reports to be reviewed and one package still sealed. The package was marked Attn: Captain Wayne Kennar, E.O. *Eyes Only.*

This is what they did to keep other agencies like the FBI or CIA etc. out of the picture as long as possible. It's not that he wanted to keep the information away from them or be the first to solve the case. It's just if he were to share information *like he's done in the past* it would take longer to get things done. Whatever you give to them, they want *you* to prove that it is not false or as they politely say "mis-information." While you're looking for evidence to the facts you know to be true the bad guys get away. They just muck things up. To many people walking all over each trying to *all* do the same job before the others do. Of course, the others are running their own investigation too and not sharing information.

The "E.O." packages were started right after they found out that an independent investigative reporter was intercepting reports in the mailroom where he was posing as an employee. Now the envelopes were tamper-proofed, and made of a material that picks up fingerprints easily.

Wayne opened the envelope and found a few of the things that he had requested. First there was a set of four mug shots of the escapees from the jailbreak. Second was a report of a white van that was abandoned in a Park and Ride parking lot. The fingerprints inside matched three of the men on the mug shots that he had. Also, they found in the van a brand-new belt that was still buckled. It had been cut with something very sharp. Prints inside the buckle matched those of Scott Glover, escaped convict. Third was a report about a body found in the trunk of a car in a junkyard. The body turned out to be that of a car salesman, who's prints were also inside the van. The drug found in his blood and around the puncture wound on his throat and chest was Insulin. Which means instant problems to a person that does not have Diabetes.

As the Captain shuffled through the rest of the paper work, his eye was caught by a report about a robbery/murder that happened just yesterday morning. 'Both owners dead and a large amount of the shelf items and frozen dinners were gone along with about six or eight coolers with all the ice in one of the freezers. More details forthcoming when the autopsy report is completed.'

Things were finally coming together. This took some of the pressure off of him. The FBI agents weren't going to be held off much longer. He was sure that they knew just about as much as he did. They would push anyway. They didn't have Carlton Bridgeman in custody either.

There were other details that he needed in order to start developing a more completed picture. He pulled out his own notebook. He now had enough to start his own list. He started this new section right below the information that came from the list that Carl let him copy from.

Carlton Frederick Bridgeman - Victim of Escapees:
brn/grn 5'10" - 31 yrs - 175 lbs - white
Amnesia [hit on head] George likes him. Foreign drugs in
system match robbery drugs.
Motorcycle owner [500 Honda] - Motorcycle over cliff on coast.
prom feature: long chestnut brown hair / green eyes
Tattoo "Rose" / Twin factor deceased

Four escapees from Ore. State prison.
Scott Glover 5'11" - 33 yr. - 215 lbs
lt.brn/lt.blu - psy. drugs req. - white prom feature: lt. blue eyes
almost colorless, white No fam. Murder of wife. [During sex, hot

springs mud bath.] Needs to be on medication (what kind?)

Rosco Wingshadow 6'3" - 41 yr. - 305 lbs Indian/Jap.
blk/dk brn. prom feature: Long black hair = religious symbol
Sister only fam. Canada
Murder of grl'frnd. ex-husb. - Gigolo X 7

Simon Tucker 6'4" - 28 yrs - 325 lbs
AKA Tuc brn/lt. brn - lt. skin = African Amer.
pro feature: 2 front teeth lg/square front upper/ others crooked
Serial murder - left 5 victims posed in public.

Gregory Stone 5'7" - 30 yrs - 143 lbs
AKA Grego prem. Bald red/blu.
pro feature: Balding red head /lg freckles.
Murder of grl'frnd - claims-innocent/framed

White van - found in park and ride near coast.
prints match 3 escapees. - belt cut, pieces in van
salesman found in wrecking yard [trunk]

Sylvia Tempest victim rape — drugs ingested through stomach and one injected after death into arm. This they knew because it was not dissolved into the bloodstream. *Matches Carl Bridgeman drug.* Dies *before* tied to Bridgman's bike / found in landslide on coast. Trace mud in various crevices of body + hair not from crash site. 3 deep scratches right arm, Blackberry thorn imbedded in breast. Cloverton area/ is a match soil and scratches match plants of said area.]

He was making his list, when another E.O. package came in. It contained information he had put in by Priority - Special Request. It told personal information about the escapees. Things that were not usually not in their personal file. This information was courtesy of a friend of his in the state capitol. 'Hmm! It seems that Mr. Glover should be on medication and has relatives not too far from here. Grandparents. I'll have to take a little trip. Maybe take Steve Smith or Thomas Walters with me. Maybe both of them. We could make a day of it. I like those boys. If I'd had son's—well anyway.'

The captain told himself, *I need to show these mug shots to Carl, and Doc needs to see this one. What am I thinking? We already saw these guys this morning in Carl's vision.* Picking up Gregory Stones picture, *I wonder if this is the guy with the broken fingers. It looks like the guy Lloyd was talking about this morning. If it is maybe we should move Carl for his own safety. Where can we put him or, is he safer where he is? At least the fed's would help protect him. They wouldn't just sit on their hands, if someone was after Carl. They are already talking like he belongs to them after he gets his memory back. It might be time to let them in on what I've got. Not turn him over, but share information. I wish I had some substantial evidence to keep them off of Carl. I'll know a lot more tomorrow after I speak to Scott Glover's Grandparents.*

# THERAPY

The "partners" were in Carl's room this morning. Carl had just relieved himself, washed his face, brushed his teeth, and climbed back into bed making himself comfortable just before they arrived. They all entered the room within a few minutes of each other.

Wayne Kennar was there. "Sorry to interrupt but before we get started Carl needs to see these and, does he recognize anyone." He spread them out on the lap table that was across Carl's legs. "Well son any of these photos ring a bell?"

"I've seen these guys in my visions and so have the twins." Carl said.

The twins agreed, nodding silently.

Doc said. "That's Charlie Cotton. I set his broken fingers. Ahh man! I liked the little guy too. He didn't seem like a criminal to me."

"I saw him in the hall right outside this room. We nodded to each other. He was outside my window, arguing with a man. Ohh God! The guy he was arguing with is this guy right here" Carl said pointing to Scott's picture. They were in the turquoise on white older model pickup truck.

"His name is Gregory Stone." Wayne said "He's a part of this group that jumped jail up in the capital. I too saw the truck outside this building.

Carl added "I can't say that I remember ever having met them. I know that they did these things to me only because of my visions and dreams."

Upon the twins' request, they all held hands together just long enough to establish a connection. Any further contact would not be necessary even days from now. The group consisted of Carl, Crystal, Ruby, Steve, Doc and Wayne. Together they had a unique connection and were prepared to see Carl through this thing.

Crystal spoke first. "Are you comfortable Carl?"

"Yes. Very much so. Thank you." He replied, and settled deeper into his pillow. He pulled a blanket up to his neck and kept his hands outside on the bed rail. Not gripping just in contact for moral support.

Ruby handed him a card.

Escalator.

All it took was the connection of five additonal minds giving him the strength he needed. Carl was once again on the hill looking toward the wall. He was just a little above eye level with the top of the wall. The distance between him and the wall was greater than he remembered from before. He had a wider view of the wall and it spread out into infinity on both ends. He couldn't even *see* the ends. Maybe there were none. Oh yes! He'd been here before all right. It looked the same. Once again as if guided by a silent request, the group of five made contact with Carl without touching him (*this would wake him*) As if choreographed, they all laid their hands upon the aura that emanated from Carl's head. Because of his injury and the chemical, there was an area in his aura just above his head that was green hued and sickly. The combined force of five was like a transfusion. Carl's body immediately felt the additional energy increase. The drain on his bodies' energy was stopped. Like discovering that the plug in the bathtub was open and then fixing it. The pull on his energy resources had stopped and the surge was enough to create the bridge that he needed.

Carl didn't even have to get on the escalator. All of his memories came flooding back to him. No small details but major events, as they truly were in his mind. Broken leg, new school, and first girlfriend all the way up to getting laid off. The bike ride up the coast, the first time he really, truly struck out on his own. This was a scary thing to him, and then before really getting anything decided about his future, or what he wanted to do with his life, he meets Harry and takes a trip down the coast trying to save the life of this stranger and himself.

Steve projected Carl's memories to the others in the room. He couldn't help himself. Carl's projections were so strong they demanded attention and this was easier than explaining what he was seeing out loud. Everyone gasped when the bike almost took Carl over the edge of the cliff with him. They all grabbed hold of the bed railing. And, gave sighs of relief when Carl had the present of mind to step off of the sliding motorcycle. Carl's thoughts leapt to himself being in the back of a pickup truck under some kind of covering and trying to move his stiff muscles. Then there were about three or four small but bright flashes of light. And then nothing, — until George woke him up in Sapphire Park. Everyone started giggling and Steve broke off with a smile of his own. They all found it difficult to concentrate with George smiling at him.

Wayne told Steve of their field trip this morning. "Tell Thomas I'm sorry. I know it's his day off but we need him to go with us. You guys meet me for lunch at my place about eleven thirty. We'll pick up some take-out and be there in about an hour. I don't want anybody in uniform. Wear jackets and vests because we'll be carrying heavy. These guys might even be there. No telling what's going on out there. The phone number was changed to an unlisted number, about a year ago. Could be, they didn't want their sweet little Scott calling collect from jail anymore."

# LIBERATION

Tuc and Grego were very excited about the car they had gone out to get yesterday. Not wanting to have it seen from the road they parked it out back behind the pickup truck. Last night when it was just getting dark, they rinsed it off with the hose. It had been sitting in the back yard of the guy that sold it to them. They had answered an ad in the paper. "MUST SELL, GOING IN THE SERVICE $350.00 OBO." They gave him three hundred, and wished him luck in the service. "You're making the right decision, going in the service. We love the Army. We've been traveling since we got out of boot camp. Seen a lot. Done a lot. Can't talk about it, special services you know. All we have is three hundred. We're in a hurry. You got the pink slip?"

They had been up since day break dusting, cleaning and packing. They'd spent some of their money on civilian clothes at the good-will.

Tuc was wearing running shoes, Levi's with a patch on one knee and a plaid shirt with the long sleeves rolled up and stretched tight over his large muscles. A belt that showed his narrowed waist. He was definitely body guard material. He tried many times to get a job, but no one would hire him. With the combination of his large forehead and crooked teeth, he scared people. He had the mis-fortune to look un-intelligent too and he knew it. He'd averaged B's and C's all the way through high school.

He avoided mirrors whenever possible. Over the years he had learned to 'blank his brain' when he shaved or brushed his teeth. His fondest wish was to get his teeth fixed, then maybe people would like him, but he had no money.

Grego found a fairly fashionable sports coat, Polo shirt, and Levi's stone washed pants. Also, black running shoes.

Their car was nice too. Such a deal, three hundred for a really nice basic Oldsmobile station wagon.

"What year is that?" Rosco asked.

"Probably about seventy to seventy-four. Who cares!" Tuc answered.

"My grand-pa, said that if the tail lights are original, the date is on the lens." Scott said bending over and looking at it closer he said. "They put it on when they mold these light covers. It's a seventy-five. This is a nice little wagon. Anything over ten years or more makes it a classic. This has only got forty-seven thousand miles on it."

"It used to belong to the kids grand-ma." Grego boasted. "It's been in the back yard since his grand-pa died, almost ten years ago. They only drove it to church and the store for years. Kid's going in the service, he needed some money. I didn't tell him that he had a classic. In this condition he could have gotten at least five thousand, maybe more. We can make money if we trade it in even if it's not running. With mileage like that it's just gettin' broke in. Tuc let's go to the gas station. I wanna check the oil, battery, transmission and brake fluids, and get gas. We don't need this little baby breaking down on the road after we get away from here."

"Nah! I'd rather stay and get things ready, so when you get back all we need to do is go. Do you think you can drive with that cast on?

"Yeah sure! This has an automatic transmission, and power steering. Not a problem. I'm right-handed and the shift handle is on the right side.

"OK then, I'll be ready when you get back." Tuc said and went back into the house.

The station wagon started up without a problem. Grego was thinking *This little beauty is actually purring. Now that it's been cleaned up some it looks rather nice, and respectful. Tuc was right about getting a used car, this one's not going to attract attention. It's dark, navy blue paint and little to no chrome trim. We do look rather ordinary.* Grego smiled with satisfaction and drove on.

Back at the house, Tuc helped Rosco put together what he was going to take with him and set it on the back porch. They were taking him to a room and board in the next good sized town that they came to. They'd pick up a newspaper when they got to town. There were usually a couple places listed in the classified ads. Somebody was always willing to rent out a spare bedroom for extra money.

Scott was leaning back in his rocking chair. He had his feet on the coffee table, and his elbows pointing in the air with his fingers locked together behind his head. Today he was an observer. This was his pad and he didn't have to do anything if he didn't want to. He was looking forward to his freedom. Deep down inside Scott was going to miss these guys. After all they had been together for a while now, more than a couple years including the time in jail. Sammy was jumpin' up and down; he could hardly control himself. *Just a little while longer. This is going to be great. Mmm! The things that we can do. The world is ours. Come-on Scott. Get up walk around, this is exciting.'* Scott was getting scared, he felt himself losing himself to Sammy's whims. It was getting to the point, where Scott could not control Sammy all the time. Sammy was getting stronger. Scott jumps up and says, "You guys got everything ready?"

"Yeah! That was the last of it." Tuc said.

"Great! Wanna play some cards or sompthin', like a going away game? It's gonna take Grego a while to get the car done." Scott explained.

Rosco and Tuc looked at each other and decided Why not? It should make the time go by faster. It always takes longer when you're watching the clock and waiting." They all went to the kitchen. Rosco says "So Scott, you going to be all right here? What are your plans?"

"Well, I'm going to kick back a while and then I'll probably get a job or sompthin'. I need to think about it for a while first like — I don't know anything for sure yet man. So many options."

+ + + + +

Twenty minutes into the game of Spades and things were getting intense. Scott was putting a lot of physical energy into throwing the cards on the table. His backside was leaving the chair — higher and higher with each discard. Before long Scott was standing up and playing cards. His chair scooted roughly back against the sink. It was his turn to deal the cards. Setting down again he shuffled the deck with a lot of flare, and offered it to be cut. While dealing the cards his energy returned, and he was standing again.

The cards were flying everywhere. It looked as if one of his hands was trying to grab the other hand and it was trying to confront the capturing hand. Tuc and Rosco slowly arose and walked backwards towards to door. Rosco backed out under Tucs' arm while Tuc held the door open for him. Tuc didn't ask. He just kinda pushed Rosco down under his armpit and behind him with his hand on top of the other man's head. Tuc closed the kitchen door behind them. They walked to where they were away from but could still see the back door, in case of pursuit.

They were unable to do anything but just stand there in the yard with their mouths open exaggeratedly wide in disbelief. It was the only way to express their feelings. They stood gaping at each other. Speechlessly incredulous at what they had just witnessed. There were no words but what they communicated to each other through their eyes was exact and understood to finest detail. *There were two people there, inside of Scott but we won't speak of it, ever, lest they would put us in the Loony Bin. Not a word ever, not even to each other — we might be overheard. We know what happened That's enough. It's enough to know, that someone else saw it too. We know that we are not seeing things that are not there, because we both saw the same thing.*

"What now?" Tuc asked staring at the back door, with the kitchen scene still on his mind.

"Well! Grego should be here soon." Rosco said. "We'll just load up and leave. When we get away from here, we should call and tell somebody about him, before he kills himself or somebody else."

Tuc smiled, still quite bewildered.

They were unaware that Sammy had slipped out of the house this morning about one AM. He had gone to an all-night restaurant and stuffed himself with foods he hadn't tasted in months. He had also driven to and from the hospital. The only thing that he saw was a man in dark blue clothes running across the park. Who would be jogging at three in the morning? Must be some kind of nut. He didn't want to talk to anyone, so he just drove back home.

When he got back to the house, he pulled into the driveway with the lights off, and pulled the truck into the garage and shut the barn style doors quietly. Using only a flash light, he walked across the dirt floor to the corner, and reached down to pull open a trap door. He descends, two flights of stairs that lead into a room that was at least twenty by thirty feet. He touched a lighter to three of the torches that were in scorched holders mounted to the walls. He stood quietly and remembered the first time he had been brought down here. And, how he always looked forward to returning. Sometimes he would even visit on holidays. There was always some kind of ritual going on, with everybody in robes that covered their naked bodies. Mmm! The girls and women he'd had while the others looked on. He was the *star* of the show.

He couldn't wait until these people left his house. Thinking how nice it was going to be at his next *real* party, he climbed another set of stairs on the opposite side of the room. When he got to the top of the stairs, he was in his grandparent's bedroom closet.

The house had been abandoned, and was waiting for the grandson to finish his sentence and claim the property. There was a special provision in their will that the property would not be seized by the government because of their grand-son's crime. Even though he inherits everything. Something about it being an accidental death. A little overzealous sex with his wife, which the judge could certainly understand even if the jury didn't buy it. A judge of influence and a very close friend to Leonard and Ellen Glover signed this document. After all the judge had enjoyed their parties too. The boy was always welcome at their functions. All three of them, were very popular at the private parties, in their hooded robes. Young Sammy was always received well by the younger members. When he had not attended, the younger members had joined the elders in their chants to make him feel their love, even if he couldn't come to them. It must be very frustrating for him not to be among his own kind. "Soon my friends! Soon!" He shouted. He would have to start making preparations soon for his *coming out* party.

*I need the only people I have left. They truly know my needs and have never hesitated to help.*

# MESSAGE

The twins' bedroom was very special. They both had their own room without a wall between. In place of the wall there was a curtain made of about nine layers of Tulle (Wedding veil material.) that was tucked and folded together. Each layer was of a different shade of the palest of blue that the eye can conceive. They had complete privacy any time they chose. Just turn on any one of three directional lights and you have instant wall and if you like, a rippling waterfall aided by a tiny fan adjusted to move the material just right. When all the lights were off at night, the fabric wall was all but transparent. To anyone that didn't know about it. It looked like a mist or pale fog. The girls walked back and forth as if it didn't exist. If you don't step between the layers of fabric just at the right angle, one would be helplessly snared. It already caught one burglar who was crying broken heartedly after being trapped there on a weekend that the twins were away. Rumors say it's enchanted. When the twins awoke at three AM., they simultaneously knew that the other was awake. They both sat up and looked at each other through the wall.

The telephone rang. Ruby answered. "Yes, Steve— It's only a warning. Calm down. — Yes, I'll put some coffee on, I doubt that any of us could sleep now. — Donuts would be nice. — We'll see you in a few minutes.

"He's getting receptive more quickly now."

"Things closer to the heart project stronger feelings." Ruby reminded her with a sleepy smile.

Crystal understood this but didn't mind being told again because it always helped to say/hear certain things out loud.

They both got out of bed and dressed for the day. They dressed casual for now. The work day didn't start until three thirty this afternoon. By the time they reach the kitchen the telephone was ringing again. Crystal picks up the receiver and says, "Good Morning Carl. What can I do for you? — Yes— I assure you it's only a warning. We'll be over there in about two hours. Wayne just got there? Oh! My! Don't let him leave until we get there. Please put him on the phone."

"This is Wayne". I —"

"Crystal here, Wayne." She interrupted. "Why are you there at four in the morning? Did something happen?"

"Carl called me. He said that the pickup truck was driving around the mini park. One of the guards went outside to get the license number. We're running it now. We have all but the last two numbers. Shouldn't be too hard to get a location. There's not that many around."

"Let's hope that it's fast. Everything is coming together really quickly. We still don't have all the pieces to plug the holes with." Crystal warned.

Wayne turned his back to everybody and lowered his voice. "Hey! I dialed your number for Carl. He doesn't know what it is."

"Thank you, Wayne. We appreciate it."

"So — what are you girls doing up this early?"

"Ruby and I were stirred by a vision. We need to see you in person. Please do not leave until we arrive. No matter what happens. Don't leave the hospital. Promise me Wayne."

"OK! You got it honey. I promise."

"Is Sara on duty tonight?"

"Yeah! She's right here. Let me put her on."

"Sara here. — Crystal? What's up."

"Listen to me carefully, *my good friend*. You are the key to saving Wayne's life. Don't tell him this, and don't be frightened. Just being where you are, at this time will, without any special actions, do the trick. First of all, don't let Wayne leave town tomorrow or rather this morning without you. You must be by his side until late this afternoon." Can you promise me that?

"Yes of course. Not a problem."

"Now give him the telephone, please. Good night."

"Wayne again— Yes that's possible. -- I'll keep her with me, I'll protect her without her even knowing it." He said quietly, behind his hand.

"She must be with you tomorrow."

Crystal, Ruby, and Steve knew it was imperative, for Wayne and Sara to believe they were protecting the other, without the other one knowing it. The vision that stirred Steve and the twins was very distinct in detail. Wayne and Sara were to stop, turn and look at each other just long enough to be missed by a flying object that would undoubtedly have taken both their lives instantly if it came in contact with them. When and where this would take place was anybody's guess. It was important to keep them together. Neither one of them knew what was to take place, just that being together was important.

It was seven thirty when Carl's breakfast tray came and broke the spell of intensity. Sara's companion guard held the door open, as the day guards arrived behind the food tray. Steve's donuts disappeared soon after they arrived. It was decided that they would all go together and get some breakfast in the cafeteria. They had a lot of work to do in the next couple of hours. They would make plans over breakfast. Everyone excused themselves and said good bye to Carl.

While they were in the cafeteria, Wayne got a call. He walked to the wall phone and got an address on the pickup from the officer that was tracing the license number. There were three vehicles and five addresses but only one that he wanted. The Cloverton, Oregon address was the same as the one they were going to later this morning. Now he had two confirmations of the same location. It was registered to Leonard and Ellen Glover. The vehicle was overdue for registration by about eight and a half months. The officer also checked and found that both owners were deceased.

+++++

Wayne had informed the FBI of the actions going down today in Cloverton. If they wanted to serve as back up that would be fine with him. This case was still under his jurisdiction via his own orders signed by his own judge down in the state capitol. The main guy they were after was a can of worms that hadn't had his medication in over a week. Scott Glover is a certified nut case. He should have been in an institution but some judge had signed a waiver that was to keep him out. The medication he was on, would be enough to control him. Just see to it that he gets it twice daily. The waiver stated that he had a seizure disorder. There was no mention of a mental illness in his record."

Among the other three escapees, no one was considered radically dangerous. Their names are:

*Simon Tucker, AKA Tuc, (rhymes with chuck) age 28 years, 325 pounds, 6'4", brown hair, light brown eyes. Afr. Amer. Serial murder, seven victims. Socially not aggressive.*

*Rosco Wingshadow, AKA none, age 41 years, 305 pounds, 6'3", long black hair, dark brown eyes. Jap/Amer. Indian Gigolo. Socially not aggressive.*

*Gregory Stone AKA Grego age 30 years, 165 pounds, 5'7", red hair balding, blue eyes, large freckles. Murder girlfriend, claims innocence ex-husband framed him.*

+++++

By ten forty-five that morning, a caravan of five cars left town, headed for Cloverton, Oregon. Two were from Wayne's group and three from the fed's. No lights and no sirens. As they pulled into the drive way an hour later, they spotted two men in the back yard. They seemed to be frozen in place, for neither one of them moved from where they stood. They just raised their hands, and stared at the house. As Steve and Thomas approached the two men, their attention was also brought to the house. Someone was arguing with someone else in the kitchen. It sounded like two men, and they were tearing the place apart.

The black man and the Indian were both mumbling at the same time. "There's only one guy in there. There's only one guy in there." That's all that they could say, over and over again. They were cuffed and taken to two different cars without resistance and put in the back seats. There was one federal agent with each, asking questions.

There were obviously two or more guys in the house. You could hear them. They were satisfied that they had all four men, so they didn't notice the dark blue station wagon that slowed down and then drove on. It turned around and parked at the side of the road.

From where Tuc was sitting, he could see Grego over the shoulder of the agent that was talking to him. He never let on that his eyes were focused on anything but the agent's shoulder. Grego waved at him with his cast, put his other hand over his heart and then blew him a kiss with a wave and a salute.

Rosco saw this. He just closed his eyes and a single tear slid down his face.

They knew that they would never see the other again.

As Thomas and Steve approached the house again, Wayne motioned for them to go the front of the house. As they re-directed their objective, the house went totally silent.

Sara and Wayne cautiously approached the back door. Sara smelled gas. She silently motioned Wayne to stop by showing him the palm of her hand and a gesture that said she smelled gas. He was about seven feet to her left. He stopped and looked at her and in that moment they both knew why they were together and fell to the ground face down. Not two seconds later the entire kitchen exploded. The oven door went sailing through the back door and between them and just inches above their heads. There was also a large section of the outside wall, half the contents of the kitchen, including knives, tableware, dishes, and furniture. If Sara hadn't signaled to Wayne, and they hadn't stopped to look at each other they would have been in direct line with the flying oven door. They both saw — in the seconds that followed a rerun that Steve was unable to stop. He and Thomas were at the side of the house and hadn't dropped to the ground. He showed them his view of the explosion and the whole outside kitchen wall on a horizontal path over their heads. They were missed by inches.

When the others in the group saw Sara and Wayne hit the ground they did likewise. It was a reaction learned in training, for the fed's and the other officers. Two of the federal cars and the patrol vans' windows were shattered but no one was injured seriously. Later there was a discovery that stunned the group. The tree right behind Wayne and Sara had a nine-inch handle-less blade that used to be a butcher knife, embedded three and a half inches into it's trunk.

Surprisingly enough there was no large fire. The small flames in the kitchen were extinguished by one of the federal officers who turned the gas off at the meter located at the side of the house. Thomas and Steve ran to assist Sara and Wayne.

There was a lot of trash and rubble to remove in order to get at them. After about three minutes of labor, it was discovered that both of them had singed hair and clothing. Both had minor cuts from flying objects including glass from the windows and dishes but otherwise they were fine. The medical team had checked them over. The paramedics and the fire department had responded to the reports of an explosion in the area.

Rosco and Tuc both had minor cuts from broken glass, and were treated on the spot. Otherwise they were OK.

The firemen and the federal officers were searching the wreckage for two bodies, when they discovered a trap door in the closet of one of the bedrooms. It was open but debris was choking the stairwell. One of the men heard sounds of movement in the area below. They began pulling debris out of the stairwell to rescue whoever may be trapped down there.

Thomas and Steve were in the yard when their attention was drawn to the garage. One of the firemen was running towards the garage. There was smoke coming out of the top and sides of the garage door also from the small window at the side of the building. Steve yells. "Firemen stop where you are." At that moment the pickup truck burst through the old wood that formed the garage door. It was backing up into the driveway. Then it lurched forward and drove around to the back of the garage. It kept going, making a complete circuit around the edge of the property. There was no way out accept the main driveway.

A mysterious good Samaritan driving a station wagon blocked it. The man had stayed just long enough to make the driver of the pickup truck get out of the truck because he wasn't going to be able to drive the truck past him. Scott tried to run for it, and didn't stop until he heard the command. *"Stop right there! Federal Officers! You are under arrest."* The warning shot brought him to a complete stop. Then the driver of the Station wagon just left.

Sammy, couldn't get away so he crawled deep into his hiding place and let Scott get out of the truck with his hands up in the air. He always let Scott take the blame for the things that he did *and* clean up the messes. But they loved each other and Scott would never betray his lover.

To the surprise of everyone, minutes later the firemen and the federal officers emerged from the garage via the trap door. "There's a chamber under the ground. It looks like there was some kind of cult activity going on down there. This whole property is sealed off until we can investigate deeper into this." The FBI agent looked at Wayne and said. "Captain Kennar we will be taking over this case as of now."

"That's not a problem. I'll finish up the paperwork and give you what I have. This will be OK with you?" Wayne said.

+++++

Ruby, Crystal and Doc were all together in Carl's room. They had experienced none of the happenings but felt that everything was OK now. They all collectively let out the emotional breath, they had been holding. Everything was going to be OK.

Carl turned the television on for the first time in two days. There was a news report just breaking. "This just in: Mysterious explosions near Cloverton, Oregon are reported, with no details as of yet. Stay tuned and we will give you updates as they come in."

+++++

Twenty minutes later. "This report just in. With the cooperation of the local area sheriff's department, the Federal Government has arrested three of the men that escaped from the Oregon State Prison less than two weeks ago. Our sources tell us that these men are responsible for the robbery and kidnapping at Carson's Pharmacy in Middleton, Oregon." Jasper Carson the owner of the drugstore is still in the hospital under guarded care. Mrs. Jasper Carson says that her husband feels responsible for his grand-daughter's kidnapping. He feels that he should have done more to stop them. "I keep telling him that he was out numbered three to one. There is nothing he could have done. He came too close to dying as it is. We both love our granddaughter. We're going to miss our good friend Maggie Penworthy too. She was the cashier that was killed during the rubbery. We've known her for more the thirty years." She was unable to say more. She just bowed her head as tears rolled down her face.

The reporter went on to say, the victim's mother is just beside herself with grief at the loss of her daughter. She had to be hospitalized after passing out when she heard the news. Reports that we have say that the Granddaughter was drugged and raped in the house that was destroyed in the explosion here in Cloverton, Oregon. Sylvia's body was found tied to a motorcycle that crashed in a landslide on the coast. Her neck was broken hours before the accident. The condition of her body, clothing and makeup fit the description of the previous victims of serial killer Simon Tucker who was arrested by federal agents just before the explosion. The agents also tell us that Carl Bridgeman the motorcycle owner was from all evidence, an innocent victim of the gangs attempt to put the blame for the girl's death onto someone else. No charges were to be filed against Mr. Bridgeman. They will be using a statement given by Captain Wayne Kennar to confirm his non-involvement. Stay tuned for our regular news broadcast at six o'clock this evening for further details.

Everyone in the room cheered and hugged each other, while tears flowed freely. No one in the room was afraid to show their feelings and when the tears dried up, they all felt stronger for the experience.

# EPILOGUE
# THREE MONTHS
# LATER—

Carl has his own apartment. As it turns out he's a very good chef. Not just a cook. A *chef*. He invited everyone over for an excellent meal. They were all having a wonderful time. Clicking his spoon against his glass Carl stands and salutes each by touching his glass to theirs and saying their name. "Crystal, Ruby, Doc, Wayne, Steve, and Sara" He said with tears that he was not ashamed of. "Words cannot tell you of how I feel towards each of you. You are now and always will be part of my life whether you want me or not. You're stuck. I'm here. I'm not going anywhere and I thank you from the bottom of my heart."

They all cheered, laughed, hugged and talked until the early hours of the morning.

Carl had his motorcycle fixed via the insurance. With his settlements from his accident policy and from his motorcycle insurance, he ended up with about nine thousand dollars. He put a down payment on a small restaurant just off the highway.

With everybody's help, and some elbow grease, Carl opened the doors for business in less than three weeks. Wayne had helped him speed up the business licenses he needed. Word spread and in the first two weeks it was obvious that he was going to do well. He even had some reservations booked for five weeks from now. He had started a policy to give away a free meal if a repeat customer brought in at least two people that hadn't been there before. "CB's Diner" was an instant success.

Sara, Carl and George became close friends.

The Twins and Carl explored his Twin factor, and to his delight Rose is still as close to him as she always was. As far as his talent goes, he is still learning. He still has that something special that makes people like him.

# EPILOGUE
## SEVEN MONTHS
## LATER

Tired after a long day in surgery, Dr. Lloyd Handle plops down heavily into the chair behind his deck. On the floor next to him he realizes, he has received a package in the mail. It had no return address on the outside. Opening the package carefully he retrieved an object about twelve inches tall wrapped in tissue.

When the tissue was pulled away, on his desk stood the most beautiful thing he had laid eyes on in ages. He knew right away who it was from. Carved out of the lightest color of woods and polished to a high gloss, were two life size hands. Both hands were palms upward, one hand cupped in the other, and together they held two new-born children. The details were exquisite right down to the tied umbilical cords, on the babies' abdomens. When he turned it around the details in the back of the hands even showed a scar that he had on his left thumb. On the base of the statue was carved in relief one word "BONUS." The piece of art was not signed and there was no letter. Lloyd clutched it to his chest, said a silent prayer recalling what the twins had said about his intuition. Thinking that perhaps there *was* a reason that he liked Charlie. This piece of art would always set on his desk. Always! *"Godspeed to you Charlie Cotton,"* he whispered.

CPSIA information can be obtained
at www.ICGtesting.com
Printed in the USA
LVHW030222260222
712053LV00001B/22